OTHER TITLES

THE ASTEROID HEAVY: *Planet Detroit*
MR. NONE: *The Salamander Game*

ADAM TRILLIONS

SEED OF THE OWL-WOLF

ADAM TRILLIONS: SEED OF THE OWL-WOLF

Published by MicroPulp Books

May 2023

This is a work of fiction. All names, places and events are entirely fictitious. Any similarity to those outside the work is purely coincidental.

First Printing

ISBN 979-8-9871466-0-6

PRINTED IN THE UNITED STATES OF AMERICA

EnviroFriendly Printing

Littleton, Colorado

www.MicroPulpBooks.com

CONTENTS

1

ASPECT
ADAM

Interior recision—Empty. Man of cold blank value and polished silver rods. The air is white, the flesh in operation. An indeterminate modulation of sterling titanium, from left to right, arising on the cheeks. The side shot and cut. The man in one direction in the epithelial soap bath:

The fiber of the weatherless tiles. The sheered reel accumulating into the otic construct perceived by the surgical ear as a voice devoid of composition: *The hour of departure has arrived. We must go our separate ways, I to die and you to live: which is better, only God knows.*

Within the anterior frame—man now stands in nine directions, a coordinate of seven, the bath above, facing a projection of withheld mind without substance.

SYSTEM: We have the prophet to exterminate religion. He will dart through the electro-magnetic field, hunted as our supreme hunter, magniloquent in self-exposure alone.

Both man and blastocyst stew gain in rigidity, the liquid congealing on the bath's endometrium lining. The man now erect, helmeted in the lustrous gray birth-brain matter from which he protrudes: *There is nothing so secret to me as the mother of pearl.*

SECURITY: The hero's virtue parallels the toxicity of our age; they constantly seek to be crowned in exile from the other.

The man and his projection; neither one nor the other.

SYSTEM: Too much insect does a clone a man make; the more illicit the trauma, the more discreet, the more contemptible its inevitable emergence—yet, to energy, we yearn.

Two versions of the man, one partial, one only realized. A composite: exinguine inapparatus.

SECURITY: To work, retaining nothing of our work, they whisper in silent transformation, this itself an observable property of Time's . . .

The man feels he has elevated the doctor he is becoming in this secret agency. Beyond rationale, the projector is drinking from a glass sun-buried in the lens of a ceph-alopod's eye: this a conjecture. The closeup is partially faceless. The evaporating shot extends out both sides of the expression, fingers displayed. The dormant tandem, lowing and lain by its stridulant focus, this body of obsessed reduction, beyond limit.

SYSTEM: I am responsible for tacit innovation. I, sensate the unreal; my interior an erythrophobic asteroid synced to the frequency of carbon. I, in the arid shadow of my blood.

SYSTEM image and man, tripling.

SECURITY: Theoretical talents am I, unborn. The idolater rectified, the unknown mirage and aspiration, the dictator divined, derived, divided from the carapace, the magnanimous sanity, I am.

Out and above—SYSTEM: a stroke of nothing. Strain, abeyance. An inverted projection of the man twice, structuralized astral space at sublime material. Operative. The man's head without corners; two surfaces occupying the same plain: the top left the top right.

SECURITY: I divide into a sickle, I dive into a cell. I tell myself that an incorruptible frivolity empowers by rendering powerless.

Out—On the left side a pool of skulls draped and projected across itself, out of itself. The man into Mankind reality postures; the projection into Mankind. There is a feeling designated by evil as *Blessedness*.

SYSTEM: Pastel bureaucracy in a dream of harrowed flesh tones; not those of human flesh, *false* human flesh.

A right-sided man, draped by a fabricated man, facsimilating an inexpensive cove of brittle glass boundaries into a triangular amalgam of intercalated bastion displays.

SECURITY: I choose not to dream, or dreams confess their fear of my mind.

A man with three left sides, expelling itself into a perpendicular man, who assays a second projection, false and sincere in the proximal encaenia of its dimensions.

SYSTEM: The facade collaborates mechanically in its formal discoloration.

Right—The man itself favored by an ethereal spider, deceiving its portion from a mantis of false precepts.

SECURITY: The living coddled adulators, mechanized and obsolete, witness the mantis who is the matrix.

East and west—Human filigree across borderline human realities; evacuated men arrested by a third party SECURITY SYSTEM; the man with fabricated surgical scents projecting himself un-christened.

SECURITY SYSTEM: Congenital endo-elaboration.

South—Humankind burdens itself into a mirror species, inaugurating a man of cloistered statehood and delicate re-semblance, who launches a contagious version of himself through a golden, basilisk-eyed monolith whenever the pillar rings. A goblet adorned with flattened cortices like miniature cybernetic elephant tongues licks the phantom fluid contained therein, emitting a lemon-hued aroma that gasps as it is imbibed. The man finds himself convinced he is a hero with a patriarchal musk. The head of cups: repro-ductive oubliettes.

SECURITY: The unknown university of the non-universe completes an electrostatic eyetooth deteriorating in a vacuum. Not a single crisis can be said to possess a greater consciousness than a flea.

Left—The man, a relic of insatiable promotion, exposed in an attitude of bristling collegiate rectitude, wound like a root around a mesmerized public pronouncing their own denouement through a cloud of unlit nosonomy.

SYSTEM: They search me as if I were their progenitor; they festoon me as if I were their professor; positions that both bore and entice me.

Right—The man tucks himself into a resonant form of a posthumous hero, the larynx of a mitigated celestial body falling through a bridge of human ash and other in-validated debris.

SYSTEM: How ponderous this hour in this constellation; how unresolved its depiction; how inept the glowering erasure the mother binds to her fabric of birth-brine salt.

Left is a minimum of three directions—the man enters from the front of the screen, with a gyrating wolf-spider the size of a dissected earlobe climbing the stalk of a marble palm tree the color and fragrance of lavender.

SECURITY SYSTEM: The true man is a bridegroom; the true nature is a bride. She will be replayed through every composition. Her analogue nature is our empery: vulnerable, splayed, vitreous.

North—The man pierced by a totemic, jewel-like birth-blood double helix of a phantasm species, inebriated by the vitality of falsehood and supremacy conjoined.

SECURITY: I am constrained, my intimate perfidy a superstition within a class of dancing neurochemist who multiply the pristine havoc of inertia; the cosmos as pristine and trans-habitable as a comedienne's cibarian oraculum.

Left—A feigned man, promenading through a series of flayed androids, as conceived as they are inanimate, a plumage of dried hawk-moth proboscises wound in thistle round each forehead, spurting saline into the vapor of catatonic Dioscuri who find themselves reaching for their bodies as they dissolve.

SECURITY SYSTEM: The intimations of lost salves, transliterated from a tincture of mercury amnesia to a sulfuric guise or gesture incubated by tainted Justice protocols, a tantalizingly barren obfuscation; here, they are a habitat for mime ingredients that remain unsolved . . . inactive catastrophes.

Right—Reflective imitation. Four cyborgs bleeding luxurious orange, teal, scarlet and burgundy eclipse oils across every wave of the solar spectrum. A fifth cyborg, with diminishing and increasing malice, discovers, spiraling in the jetty of its own intestines, the detached porcelain finger of a deceased sixth cyborg.

SECURITY SYSTEM: To care not for the heart, to manumit order as a proximal gelatin, a by-productive vestal coercion, is anarchy's most obsequious form; need not interrogate . . .

A theorem of apostate sequence—A cyborg silently disgorging its aeronautical bile onto a pristine vista yet to appear. The silence after the screams of an entire race. The mask is the engine directing itself. Quaking water as thin as its reflection upon the sensor. At this moment there is no *in* or *out*.

SECURITY SYSTEM: Despotism is the media curated by trans-magnetic agents; propulsion dolls astride the informant like a horse, disemboweled by the creditor, auditor, or practical violence polymath.

The General, a flesh bacteria composited onto a dwarf's frame, prodding his depleted, phlegm-like rolls with an eagle talon bundled in discarded neurons, his bladder spraying onto his skin-colored khakis from a dichroic orgone-accumulating replica of his own face hidden in his navel.

SECURITY SYSTEM: I am the champion of all embalming credulities.

Man and General turn from one another or into one another.

SECURITY SYSTEM: For my audience only beasts, contraindications, porous quasars, and integrated pairs.

The General opens his pituitary mouth to reveal the Hero, vertical in the shell of a salamander's egg, a single drop of molten iron running down his spine, this metempsychosis spilling a year's worth of flushed, incorporeal laurels through negative charges without time.

The General: Slowed cuticle, the ageless eye, The amber waves deranged; The purple mounds of amputees, Convex, denuded planes. Comerica, Unmerica, Who spays thy debt for thee? The fulsome crown, shorn widowhood, From sleep departing   seep.

Cut.

2

THE PROMETHEUS CLINIC

Probe lights. Orbital. Proscenium.

Architects of the Syncorp Incubator: the corpulent General Thrasyllus Hating; the mantis-like Dr. Tiresias Goldwater; Io, the Bionic Venus. The reconstructed Adam on a weaponized operating table.

Gen. Hating: I have prayed to be the only being with power in this galaxy. The rest of you, gathered here to mark the passing of this ceremony—the momentary sum of my endeavors—are but reflections of myself and the boundless atrocities I deem worthy enough to provide the metabolic relationship of my illumination. *Quos vult perdere dementat.* I abominate and dispose of my abominations without furthering the pressure on my auxiliary aorta. I have never been interrupted. A single drop of adrenal fluid sparkling on a silver thread of silk protein. We, my slaves and my selves, are at the center of the spider's web: this is our compass, depending on which end of the skin you drink from. Is something teaching a newborn to cherish the humility of starvation? The time is the year 1973. 1010. 0. 84. 911. We begin again, now, with this whimpering body we are parsing to christen, after having etherically estimated it—our preferred means of reforming the carnal vehicle to our image, to *my* image—this my newest child before me admonishes: and so the exterminator enters the experiment in the grand tradition.

Dr. Goldwater: The object will be subjected to non-bias upon introduction. Grief at the "loss" will be anomalous or nil. Io assures this.

Gen. Hating: I am in my Prometheus aspect to honor these hallowed proceedings, to celebrate the appearance of this ancient technology to the world as it manifests in the guise of ADVANCEMENT. We have been here before, we will be here again, we have been here FOREVER. Boredom alone is my nemesis and my surety of pleasure. Boredom, the self-immolator, the cannibal sensation with profligate tendrils of gray, impermeable meat. Let it be known that I am the sole individual engineering these declarations, that with every god both named and nameless inside me I've come as the conqueror to perform my tiresome office, to devour each new dawn before its conception.

Dr. Goldwater: You have indecipherability. Can it be derived from your truth how the truth is often more deceptive than deception?

Gen. Hating: These are the most tremendous games one can play: to manipulate with one's own will the genetic material of predetermined civilization to the point of final extermination as a sacrifice to one's own will? I demand a bolder deficit, a more ecstatic amelioration! This tepid formula of Ex-determination; that is when I have been absorbed into the whole, the predator complete; that is when I will be finalized *in* what I have conquered. I have been finalized times without number. Chaos assimilation?

Simpering, lusterless, tone-deaf and uniform; docile, credible counterparts to an outstripped pulse of embryonic plastic shade. The natural futility of the polluted. The mysterious rigor we've exerted to attain our grand *Synthesis Fatale* is an offer of erasure to all classical *Praedicamenta*. To my hip the sword, my illusion the assassin! Time melts like mother's milk . . .

Dr. Goldwater: That depends upon which end of the spider you drink from . . . An obliterated metronome, any way you serve it, obfuscates much, but never cacophony.

Gen. Hating: You, in the guise of yourself, adduce maxims as unknown as they are complete. So shall your voice be written.

Dr. Goldwater: On the voice of the wind the voice of the chimera propagates . . . on the voice of the assembled machine, solicitous of war, glory, the renowned hazards of holy honor and martial distinction. Shall we inhabit it?

Gen. Hating: So many deaths for so many bouquets, so many petty prodigies divulged in the light of the sun in a flat universe where Dr. Tiresias Goldwater, the signifier of the yet more elite Dr. Tiresias Goldwater, signified. The feast of the evening includes the faces of who we were, who we might have been, who we might be, who we have the potential to become, and who we *will* become. You wish you could see the face of who you are. Alas, it has been consumed by that splenetic community of revolution. That is what the correlative designed in other dimensions will violate and trump. Such auguries flood the spirit with the restorative vigor of an impending cataclysm.

Dr. Goldwater: I am to inhabit a white star, but first it must be built, and there I meet myself again, for my hands must build it.

Gen. Hating: Our clone race traces its lineage directly to Caligula. A sense of vulnerability, invulnerability, and elasticity renders us deleterious, incomprehensible. Yet when I posed as the Carpenter and became the Walrus, the commanding inamorata of the species saw me in a dream later deemed oracular, inscribing upon the bars of their cages as well the cells of their blood: *We have led the guests this far, why must they now turn to children? Why must they author such mangled suicides of prayer?* The farce has no recourse but to torture itself. What familial completion we will purge into its enigma after the inevitability has dissolved. At the apex, we will destroy all evidence of transmission: of him, of us, of the void.

[Dr. Tiresias Goldwater *finds himself convinced that* Time *has been set back in honor of this stupendous man* General Nianthimedes "Thrasyllus" Hating. *Everything is re-beginning.*]

General Hating: I am in my Prometheus aspect, the Emperor of Maladies. The vultures I have sent to devour the death-image of antimatter devour my liver. They are my slaves. They lick clean the stitches I have woven round the sun to seal it in Space. There is a body upon the table before us, still skinned in white nothingness. We have consecrated the outline, subatomic threads of bruised pastel gaining substance, and now it seems that at last the completed anatomical mechanism will materialize. The quasar opens and no one notices the impending penumbra.

Seeding Blastocyst Stew with Caligula Particle Mystery Images revoked: the empty cold blank value of Man. The man can prove nothing to himself of the Saturn black-matter wine harvester, the self assembling metallic vine grid virus, Eolus' brain, the Warp Office, Head Cam. *Do you suppose God will look upon us as guiltless while we, motionless, behold these things?* Man: empty cold blank of value. Somewhere in the corners of White Space the pod is detonating. The fragmented human seed body—the one trillionth clone imbued with the mercurial capacities of the Caligula Particle—falls endlessly across a directionless plane. Time, still clinging to the matter of the body that brought it here, becomes confused by the separation of limbs and internal organs, registering discretely for each, reversing. At the center of the strewn anatomy the brain, in three pieces, whirls like a triad of disjointed moons: *I was traversing White Space.*

Io opens at last to exhale her impending precision: *No one noticed how I was tormenting impossible magnitudes, uploading imported magnetisms . . . That mantodean beggar, the thousand-eyed infidel, the thousand-tiered deficit, Dr. Goldwater Tiresias, fled in persecution to the unlimited cliff-sides where he found me chained. Impostor! His promotional toxins lain in a tablet as fathomless as the night in my blood! I am the victim of his generosities, the young woman who dashed out of her own throat before her words, those blazing chariots of incandescent crystalline gold, conduits of meticulous stratification devoid of embrasure, erased in variety, the watch un-maker undressed as the day by a riverine eclipse, yet still clothed in scraping clean fissures faster than the receding tongue: the searing, immutable networks committed in the mouth's margins; the receding dissolving; the captive legs and their captivated shadows, the festering longing enslaved to release. Should the human race permit itself the constant shifting of identity?*

Dr. Tiresias: The corpses are wrapped in music and every sound corresponds to a color. Youth is a cataract opening into a game. Your position is synonymous with the gestures staged by the light, granting the observed the sole derivation of significance. The early age of the idol is fission. That is why reason has to become *one,* an infeasible vision, yet exchange is best for the senses, wouldn't you agree?

Gen. Hating: The contract stipulates the old opulence to resemble the Lords of Laboratory Limbo. The weak abhor what they change as they change into it for their terror to abate.

Dr. Tiresias: To search purity for the despised superstructure of accounting.

Gen. Hating: To file or be defiled.

Io: If the generic articles of prodigality accumulate artificial wealth, does this abate their functional abhorrence?

Gen. Hating: Every General must be left their region of lawlessness: this is where they practice their basic mono-timbre-isms and encryption.

Dr. Tiresias: Women are codes of gamma-battery and neon, thus they are impervious to the electrical prodigies of covalent corruption while remaining its material stimulus.

Io: We must substitute the mind with a weaker object if it is the mind we wish to escape.

Dr. Tiresias: A volatile moment of futility manumitted into total frivolity: two poles oscillate, extract. *If only the president had isolated me as an embryo,* the woman says, *I wouldn't have this monumental complex of tangled fetuses I call my Soldier's Instinct.*

Io: Compensation for the minuscule inverter of the size as can be seen. You and this porcine magnate must valve the value of your premonitory Venusian massacre masquerade.

[Climates unseen, devolving in the uterine sunlight.]

The body has been addressed. In a fortune of ideal euso-cialism it must be a querulous success. No one is breathing. The water-clock of the future reveals the chest to be converted, the transparent heart the X-Ray of a pneumatic isopsephy. The Self has been preserved as an illustrious trope extinguished by the background radiation of this inter-dimensional banking executive's infirmary. Adam has been assembled, on the head a garland of exploitation to be acquired through the rigors of physiological dismemberment in every temporal field as empirical simultaneity permits. Re-assembled.

Io: I see the symbol, the flared iris expanding like a collapsed star.

[*The mandatory entrance of a standard* ORDERLY.]

ORDERLY: A black hole is in fact an atrocious birth canal. We call it a 'poverty mine'. The families there get poorer and poorer until they're at last so stupid their faces crowd together with every face ever forgotten. This man was their audience. Now he's an unconscious half-caste in the failing light, and you are all actors, all but me. I am more powerful and wiser than even my most extensive self-actualization.

Dr. Tiresias: His blood has withered in the star-generator. As each day grows less dazzling, so in the new combinations of his blood, its letters and balances, its charge, his eyes grow brighter.

Io: Though you see, you are blind.

Gen. Hating: Though you have a thousand incorporeal eyes, you have not seen a black hole.

Dr. Tiresias: The Universe has misinterpreted my soul. The Fates have threaded the Universe wrong. Here, in this ocular clearance, my loveless ruler manifests insular externality: independent nodes of a nonexistent process.

Io: Before Heaven and Earth there was but one visage: its seeds were perpetual.

Dr. Tiresias: Plutonium glowworms hidden in the syrinx.

Gen. Hating: They were made in my image. I have appropriated the holy fire from Jove. Now I recompose it: a cylinder to be consecrated by a flat circle.

Dr. Tiresias: Building money is more expensive than using it to deny it. This is an excellent opportunity to consult perpetual immolation.

Io: Malpractice reeks of odorless lavender, if you would care to notice; air smells like a vacuum, before silver dissolves it.

Dr. Tiresias: Coherent pleas, gold conducted through the thin golden wire of malfeasance.

Gen. Hating: This is the embodiment of applause for government assistance initiatives post programming. The lions offer their subjects their absent insecurities. They'll toss their children into the air to be caught in the jaws of levitation while they formlessly graze.

Io: *Blessed Other . . .*

Dr. Tiresias: . . . cold industry, fashioned from the shape of a thought-second in an appetite abolished. [*The steel rods are grown over by flesh, the current drives them. Attenuation. Influx. Actuation.*]

Gen. Hating: Now he and she and thee are me and I am twice the encomium of a fingerprint, twice the common autocrat's Time-vehicle.

Io: When will we learn this?

Dr. Tiresias: We must aggrandize our superior's capital lethargies if we wish to become immortal.

(*Pause.*)

[Pause is the essence of betrayal.]

Io: Earth is the homogeneous planet: it's got everybody on it.

Gen. Hating: And yet I squander humanity, to weave my assignation with the blow of a toneless kiss.

Io: On the body-centric profane metaphysical level I fear I am vigorous enough to return to my wavering. Where are my friends? I loathe them until they cease wanting me. Thus are the vicissitudes of tissue culture.

Gen. Hating: Will you again summon penury? Stimulate a tumor? Simulate a vaccine for horror, passion, vanity? Your confessions portend themselves; your nervous animation elects to pretend itself mute, too beautified to possess even obvious beauty, to beatified to possess beatitude.

Io: Too sterile to possess even obvious sterility.

Gen. Hating: The law is omnipotent. I don't recall giving you permission to believe in one size or the other.

Io: It's what I should think I was taught I would say I could think I should do.

Gen. Hating: I should think your fur coat requires an attorney.

Io: That's what I'm thinking for you. It's jaguar . . .

Dr. Tiresias: As quickly as the destitute grow she shall grow destitute . . .

Io: Flourish and preside . . .

Gen. Hating: Your retracted mineral ions a mask no man can see . . .

Io: Phantoms quickly lose their charm, as she recalls.

Gen. Hating: Obsolescence deposes both physical charm and physical strife.

Dr. Tiresias: Arrhythmia adorns her vision as her heart is strained.

Gen. Hating: Her voice is.

Io: The rest can be summarized as functional illusion or quantum protocol. Let's assemble for her the infinite and guide her to the slaughter . . .

Dr. Tiresias: Her bile is prejudice: it alludes to judgment.

Gen. Hating: She is our guest.

[Adam quivers/stirs/?]

Adam: We are all guests.

Gen. Hating: As long as I dictate the theater of battle I will produce sublime panoramas.

Adam: Would you like to trade some of your clairvoyance for the minimax theorem of total recall?

Io: He is but the guest of his own iridescent shadow, his own invisible presence.

Gen. Hating: That's relative, or immoral. Such tactics are their own analogues.

Io: Your deceit is an inspiration to the half-born.

Gen. Hating: She is no longer to be honored, nor dishonored.

Dr. Tiresias: Her own untarnished system is merely that: a system.

Gen. Hating: Her womb an automat of Bayesian Belief Networks.

Dr. Tiresias: The Human Frequency Control Signal.

Gen. Hating: A cybernetic children's illustrator.

Dr. Tiresias: The Whole Earth Catalog.

Io: Exotropic time.

Gen. Hating: Cosmetic discord. Antepraedicamenta. Simulation is a procedure we must assimilate to simulate.

Io: He wearies of the correct delusion.

Gen. Hating: You are either a joke, or your own mime.

Dr. Tiresias: Mechanical entrails lucid and calculated . . . how shall we suborn her infantilism?

Io: Why?

Gen. Hating: These insipid liminal constructs obsess me . . .

Io: If you are employed as the legal representative of your own self-abnegation . . .

Dr. Tiresias: You are but an illusion projected onto yourself by your own mind.

Io: Have I decided to allow you to let me make that decision? My personal liberty facilitates both exits and entrances, a circumstance of self-emulation. I am a revolving theater of Self.

Dr. Tiresias: Hence it must be ignored. An emollient of fetal anemia is mixed in her vinegar, then the queen ant peels apart her salpinges.

[*Hieratic silence.*]

Io: I celebrate the birth-mite.

Gen. Hating: How fetching.

Io: Pseudo-science is a science.

Gen. Hating: Besides, how much did you eat of it?

Io: All. All but the lips.

3

OPERATION TRIVIA

Fall. Estuary. Oil.

Adam: Spring is in the perfection of the blood, the blood of water and sentient oils. It is the scent of a fetus in reverse and the things we can't imagine.

Io: This is why I am here with you, in the crocus and the iris, in the cypress and the orchid, because spring is imperfect, even encapsulated in a honeycomb, even where we lay in the sunflower on the rotary of the Divine Will. The branches reach through exposure, the sun elongated upon the beasts it has stifled.

Adam: The tamarisk, the eucalyptus and the olive live vicariously for us. It is their hypostatic eggs the river coils over the earth.

Io (*a maggot of phosphorus dislodging from her lips*): It laps at my lips from a cup of my own hands.

Adam: The dirt lives every life, it lives forever. It is an organ vaster than any worm or any serpent, more serene than any spider.

Io: My mind is a spider ravening its way through a cocoon of inutile sonar, a quagmire of lichen and stones burning coolly in a hive of drowning quail, adenine and thymine.

Adam: We lay in the tern's nest with the putrefied locusts.

Io: These are our provinces.

Adam: Where we achieve the quantum of motionlessness.

Io: Peripheral apparitions liberated from order and style . . .

Adam: And the taste of our libation bearers . . .

Io: Vestiges unmitigated, silent in our dance . . .

Adam: Our conundrums mistaken for song . . .

Io: In this empery of radioactive horizons, eclipses and virtual twilight . . .

Adam: They serve to recite our threnody . . .

Io: Expiring with the arrival of the spectators, ornamented with nothingness . . .

Adam: You reach into expiration for the featherless bird in its human agony of crystal . . .

Io: Its crystalline hide raw secretion, purged of inheritance . . .

Adam: All but for the atomic glory it purchased . . .

Io: The carapace engineered from the bio-productive forms of sequence . . .

Adam: Human again, made in atonement . . .

Io: The undying pain of innocence . . .

Adam: Some believe even that to be a currency.

Io: It holds a current.

Adam: As do the screams of the native doubles in their ameliorated constructs.

Io: The spider's web a salival bridge between the thorns of mechanical pressure and the hemochromatosis of an ever-lasting autumn, the onslaught of a million imperishable butterflies mystically reverberating.

Adam: The spider on a thread of crescent moon calls its milk-tongued plague to account. A number that can't be counted bodes of impermanence. The force of iron against the silver planet-light and terrene blush, where the Fates uncurl faceless edicts onto the winter's pyre, the pellucid cornea where the story never comes, where I stand un-fettered, this embryonic dimension as always an unknown fruit to forget, a stasis to re-compass, a sky of citrus melting like hot glass swallows the statues of a floating catacomb, the first and final darkening of a tactile absence surrounding us at the pool's bottom, this spurious and irremediable un-left-behind.

Io: We attest to the incomplete nature of our biologies.

Adam: Our flawless rivals, their flawless brutality, their decimated antidotes . . . Stop motion.

{*A* SECOND *is born, indistinguishable from the* FIRST}: The order of order, escape! This garden is the location trivia of the lower trophic protist wage, a pristine species of non-soil and identified wishes.

{*The* FIRST *is born*}: Here we ready to work, again and again, our reduced problems proliferate, always leading to work, an appetite without hunger, from inside the belly of the world, without succor, at last I am beheld as truth as I behold the truth, the cosmos as frail as an evanescent string of star-like protozoa, pulled in every direction by the darkness of God's mind.

Second (*Eido-Omega*): My opinion is depleted as I talk, so it is right, as I have the right to do so.

Io: Inviolable quietude is for the blessed, even as surely as the unlearned recognize this.

Eido-Omega: In here there is no one to be me, so I am here to see no one, but yes.

Io: Arise, without your wages.

Eido-Omega: Despise the fact. No, I have a tenebrous concentration of all I have inside me.

First (*Eido-Enoch*): No, I have the gratitude of my anatomy, of a second anatomy I have the most of inside the gradations of my own gratitude.

Eido-Omega: A considerate station. Altruistic. The alternating current of my perspective is the only truth beneath me.

Adam: The truth of evolution? Of gold? Of Godhead and Empire? Of silt encrusted mercury? Brain matter? Fermentation? The populace? The wetness of rain? The doomed still waiting to be bred? The anaerobically chaste?

Foreign investment? Changeling fatherlings and the bright fiddler of the occident? The noble incipient sloth? Formation commodities? Star-tombs decanted with the rationale of a *cordon sanitaire*? A strained and forsaken lineage?

Eido-Omega: This is the address of the foundation: a zero-point magnesium flare, a formulaic continent.

Eido-Enoch: It is our duty to remain surveilled.

Eido-Omega: Would you say you are my student?

Eido-Enoch: The answer is me.

Eido-Omega: You will find I am made of cross-cloud.

Eido-Enoch: Your scourge a diagnostic anxiety.

Eido-Omega: Potent.

Eido-Enoch: Begin the granule, begin the strife of payment, begin the ultramarine.

Io: Not in the mist. The heart is still very tender as a de-compartmentalized object of contrition.

Eido-Enoch: A minus-clock grafted onto the annals of motion.

Eido-Omega: Waiting in the-water-of-twenty-years-ago to go.

Adam: If I am to substitute myself for myself post-critical, cancellations remark the effect this neutralized breath-taking has on my adamantine physique.

Eido-Enoch: The spoiling momentum of uninhabitable sunlight.

Eido-Omega: Get me the anomaly! The hemato-sensory of a liver digested by the oil of fledgling procedural convection!

Eido-Omega: (*Opens their stomach to remove an undiscovered kingdom of vitriolic docility, a collage of all temples and organs motorized by decree of* Hermaphroditus, *rising from the center of the image.*) I won't become you. I am only my religion and I am my only religion. The name of this rite is *Genuine Contempt Masquerading as Manufactured Contempt.* I produced it for the stage of years-to-go. Is that why I am hated, because I am the essence of beloved?

The room, a staccato burial mound slotted with the history of modern warfare, an ancient nest of metaphysical espionage masked as compounds of immotile elements, succumbs to the philodendrons.

Adam: We find the history of appearance illuminating. Let us gather each view unto declension, then exit through the life that you have done so.

Io: Genetic knowledge in its primary has been wounded, embedded in the worth of looking upon this as I was before I saw.

Adam: Pride statutes of an intervening republic: the halves and the have-nots. This is why your questions have turned into loopholes.

Io: The be-haves have not: a fountain of interlocking universes dismembered at the hemato-nuclear inter-cessation.

Eido-Enoch: Cast your gaze upon the story of a father, the master-theorem of the titular Owl-Wolf King, the King of Puppets.

[*A tracery of molecular mezzotints, a neurasthenic murmur*]: I've read the puppets. They have and they do not. The fake monitor is real.]

The Mother of Puppets addresses the fatality of war: *The puppet strings are tied asleep to home. On him his body creeps downstairs, to the tearful bore giving remission their strings. The end is real.*

Adam: To some.

Io ignites the second. Outside, the last dove of the dying world: *The proper flesh now for you. What is your name?*

Eido-Enoch: I was a child in seething compression, sound-less as remembrance. But the flash burn on the melting water?

Io: Conception.

Adam: Cathexis.

Eido-Enoch: I appeal to the submission of genetic distortions.

Io: If you pledge the deaf must-have-been.

Eido-Enoch: I have no brain, but an intricate gem-like surface.

Io: Then we should.

Adam: Friends, when would you stay quiescent?

Io: It is the only privilege.

Adam: *<How would you think chemopause?>*

Io: Would taste, if it were parting with its tongue?

Eido-Enoch: Have you considered how I will retain myself?

Io: With proposal. With sponsored bifurcations replicating the vortices of an infernal picture plane.

Eido-Enoch: Every sign-language proposed by what is not a real person. I am only everything that is a total.

Adam: I am only the everlasting circumstance of private purity and perfection, the subject of matter realizing itself with a shock, the personification of a political *too-ephemeral-to-generate* amplified beyond de-individuation.

Eido-Enoch: In the astral boardroom the citizens are witnessing a pageant of organic atoms meld pre-time onto a circuit of cosmic anti-blood.

Adam: In this echo of vegetation the flame of life stirs its web, stirs the dungeon of every shadow with coolness.

Eido-Enoch: There are no collected pedestrians to depreciate the poetry of everyone, the philosophy of the world, the folk wisdom of everything.

Adam: As it is we're having the power of primordial industry bestow upon us a contact with the demi urge of hagiographic apex, trans-stellar emanation. This vision is filled with providential soul.

Io: An agreement transmuting the genetic fibers of the hibiscus, the gordian banyan and the willows, from generic facsimiles of ultimate detail into singular unwithered icons teeming with the mercurial sinew of lost time in a time that never was.

Adam: The costumes pass into the people of reality. We must celebrate our children, not by modifying their appearance on a sub-molecular level, unless it is with the candlelight of our eyes reflecting off the fountain palms and the birds of paradise.

Io: In the latent aura of early-fashioned plains enveloped in verdure I exude the feminine thought which asks, *Will this be our place?*

Adam: Will it be ours for too long, or to long for?

Eido-Enoch: Then we shouldn't have tried. Maybe hesitating will help . . .

Adam: Who?

Eido-Omega: The vivisector will never taste the factory that is building out of the interstices. It will never be built and it will be here because we'll never build it.

Eido-Enoch: I would love to one day find myself a daylight factory, vivid as the first fact. I would allow myself the position of supervisor, in an uncanny vision draining the well of retraced fortune . . .

Eido-Omega: . . . with a payment of retroactive loss. That is the lot of monetary tri-monadism.

Eido-Enoch: The umbel taste of the helioptic nerve outspreads the black-hole of value-thought.

Eido-Omega: The bitter taste of the baseless ideas tastes better.

Zero-zenith.

Mandate: The think-no-concepts beset with reaching their surrogate of functionality become no-factors. It happens when the Associative World Agreement detects all facial trans-volition of the mutable verifiable parity-plethora. Photo-conceptive appendices hyper-balance at vertex of discharge.

Eido-Omega: The discharged mind must be articulated, the articulated mind insured.

Eido-Enoch: Was our first purpose to aspire to a purpose? Will this complete continuity?

Adam: A hydraulic awareness in a unified likeness.

Io: A collection of scented ointments resembling a cove somewhere in calypso-time.

Eido-Omega: The courtroom a skull aerated by scorpions, the set embarked on by all tourists.

Eido-Enoch: It is our passion to bankrupt and to be bank-rupted. For mercy we ask a needle.

Io: My love is what I ask my love, items of mania obligated to meaning, manipulative control over everything yet annihilated.

Adam: The droning stagnant buzz of long ago, the long ago to come, stratified, uncalibrated, re-made by anything you find there.

Eido-Omega: As you were.

Adam: By me, as I am, the selections re-divided, discovered no pardon.

Io: My voice of Eden I start pacing, but these behaviors can operate themselves.

Adam: A mincing effect, to think of the menace that lies in the roots of the universe beneath the word *menace*.

Eido-Enoch: If we keep aging paradigmetically we'll get chastised while we're young, then do half as much labor without the gain of a thousand benefits.

Eido-Omega: Though our salary will decline as expected, do you know what I'm going to offer our host? The skeleton of a hiss denoting its seams most paused.

Eido-Enoch: The ultimate humor.

Adam: Uninhabitable sunlight.

Io: A membrane over a discrete palate.

[*A severed artery examined for the best view, re-contextualized in contrast.*]

[*Diurnal dwindling in the* Garden of Even.]

{Descent. Estuary. Oil.}

4

COLONY JUPITER

A stage of eons.

In this room everything is acquired, that's why it is here: objects remain in the color natural to the bereft, the will of a body previously scanned. The three systems: General Thrassylus Hating, Dr. Tiresias Goldwater, Io, cast from one corner to the other. The three Monitors: platinum striates their legs, oozing from their bones from wounds they will never dress. They look at me as if they recognize they are being used. I assure them that it is so, that they will never regain all they have lost, all they are losing, all they have yet to lose, from one end of the room to the other. All they have is a simple glare they call *Virtue*.

I abstain from all systems. That is how I remain my constantly emerging autotype, reinventing the Jupiter base from the wires in my cheeks. Would you pose as me? *Behold, I seek not for power, but to pull it down. I seek not for the honor of the world, but for the glory of my God, and the freedom and welfare of my country.* Would you threaten to pose as who you are? *I am constantly victorious,* says the General. *It is the year of escaped blood, an idea that democratized fearlessness.* The logical terrors escape my blood. They rejoin me. They re-evaluate their tendencies. *Trillion dollar babies and I have a day of such vivid ultimation the darkness turns white as an opal,* my old nemesis Thrassyllus of Mendes predicted.

Dr. Tiresias: We loaded him with too much information. Now he is simply a residual intruder.

Io: I can't find him.

Adam: There is another country inside me, aside from the one you abandoned like a skeletal prelude to a perpetual increment.

Io: We can live away from the world in the forest, where the crops raise themselves, and dress like we were never-born.

Adam: God will not suffer that we should perish with hunger; therefore he will give unto us of your food, even if it must be by the sword. Now see that ye fulfill the word of God.

Io wants me to synthesize a platitude of error for her clinician's ego to calibrate. She seeks an immediacy of normative association, shorn, distilled, which I suggest she abstain from, knowing her refusal to data-feed earth-subjects a final integer-source.

Adam: If a bigot were to descend from Aeneas, I would prefer to hold it in off-embrace rather than force my mouth into the tautological post-protocol.

Dr. Tiresias: Nature procures such infamies as only a sizeless hierophant can predict, with his cithara's excrement of pearls. Io subjugates her lipless smacking to the last sphere of interest. This must be what she means by *weaponized purity and perfection.*

Adam: Tenth generation sub-systems don't have a prophetic frequency or any other evaluative strictures: Courage, Insight, Power...

Gen. Hating: He has the normal imbalance, thus he represents the commonplace.

The General suckles his scotch like a stuck pig fetus breathing sour camphor on a mammary of corn. The scene endures. Opposite Io, the prurient Dr. Tiresias cries, faints, balds, incapable of a satisfactory collapse.

Gen. Hating: You are aggrandizing cultural perception, you hormonal beast. You have discovered the discovery of nothing, something that will forego the sanctity of an embolism. The reivers are here to operate their empathy, but for all that, cannot exist.

[Gen. Hating *removes an ear. The walls sink back into their folds as if exhausted. The will of* Time *is unable to clasp itself shut around its unmitigated circumference. The smell of corn fills the arid golden expanse like microwaved sunlight. The floor beneath is human, impermanent, charged with scab-pink voltage and scrubbed of all abrasions. The windows are calloused, their frames composed of mutilation. The chancres have scurried away. A black geyser splits open the ceiling, nets of toes sweetly trickling down from weeping* Space. *Io abdicates her mimetic blood. Low on the* Earth *a dark bloom spreads, to the splendor of* Dr. Tiresias' *masticating. A fetus uncurls in a ball of pink lightning, absorbed by the black spire of* Gen. Hating's *ion cannon. The illusion stops under the magical pressure of its anfractuosity.*]

Dr. Tiresias: This is limbo magic.

Gen. Hating: What luck.

Io: Here come the yeomen with their illicit dualities and famine.

[*Peonies inflate in a celebration of brevity and satellite sensations. The day known as the* Circumscription of Rhodopsis *passes over. Pardons are begged and justice is flayed.*]

Adam: This is all a lie. There is no course for the truth in this summary of hallucino-gentrified tragedy types and their stillborn aromas. The faceless portending of neurological drone-mancy is a particular spell cast by ice-captured phoneme-paced moths soundlessly muttered beside this counter-incantation of the angiosperm vacuum: *anything I want is all I want,* which seeps like a new zygote passed the inaccessible petulance of the commander and his demons of sterility, penetrating the living nature like an ox horn through a cloud of smog, one after the other, till at last a swan's neck protrudes from a rat's leg at breech birth; the method is taught as Scamander.

Dr. Tiresias recites the verdicts of his pleasure: *The truth of anyone's behavior is the truth of everyone's behavior, thus she spoke. To prod a lilac with the ring-finger-like branch of a dominant corpse is the dead finch dripping from your mother's mouth, the mule's eyes simultaneously spoiling in a pit of caviar.*

Gen. Hating: I have to call an old friend.

Dr. Tiresias: Explain to him our predicament, that should suffice as an example of crime.

Gen. Hating: We were warned.

Dr. Tiresias: The spell of a new machine is very potent.

Gen. Hating: Implant a subordinate uterus in the heart's left atrium then graft the heart onto the exterior liver. That comes straight from the top. Bake it all in sand. You must then give birth to a spider mite masquerading as a water witch at a senatorial debate, and your offspring must inject you.

Dr. Tiresias: I can see the logic in these worrisome super-impositions, however, their critical mass may impede the strike.

Gen. Hating: I've tried to dismiss all I've told you, remain completely objective.

Dr. Tiresias: I submit my infallible retention.

Gen. Hating: Curl up with your incentive in a generator. When you finally crawl out, the world on the face of the Earth could be nothing more than a pristine void deline-ated from the sky by shelves of electronic vapor.

Dr. Tiresias: It is the will of the Universe I cannot reproduce.

Gen. Hating: Or mass-produce.

Dr. Tiresias: And abode in discontent to the proper obeisances of your order.

Adam (removing his ribs of carved garnet, his spine of sardonyx and gold, his eyes of carmine antimatter): My blood ranges out through the red and white filaments of insoluble gas, the glove-like low mercury fission. It must want my teeth to constrict the unthinkable damnation I report to myself, in a speculative cloister of dental superstitions known as my fauna. My eyes run down my cheeks, like two man-o'-war released from their thermohalinic cages, to say, at last, that is all the evidence I can present.

Gen. Hating: Combining regrets is over.

Dr. Tiresias: Io coddles twilight between the shelves of a sidereal hologram. This volatile clockwork of the immaterial may out-spread the horizon, its veneer of mountain-like paleo-beings and non-beings rehearsing their vestiges.

[*The pulse of every point deflating, scales ringing out from every wrist: this is the indivisible circumsolution concluded, the honor of horror* Gen. Hating *has not failed to account for, to take into the figures of his monuments as they arrive at realization. There is no riposte to be excised, nor the enmity of a necessary and trivial fraud: instead, the light licks away the search for Justice, wasting none of its saliva on the macro-fibrillation of* Law.]

Io: Erigyius declares to himself the poured wine in the anatomy of vision.

Gen. Hating: Integrate Larichus Protocol into the synchronized quibbling. For Charaxus, reset Doricha.

Dr. Tiresias: Our lord Jupiter re-posits himself as his sister, Juno. This cauterizes our essences: they feel as if they've unfastened as they became. Everything has been wiped, blank, in blindness it suffers the salvation of neither freedom nor ethic. This allows impermeable libraries of provisional consequence to starve, to reprimand the deeds we now pursue not on our own, nor with others who belong to any arch-disseminated vulture-caste without our consent.

Adam: Since the day I was manufactured into birth I have protected these demands to be ingested before my pyre, with the words I say standing beside me, conflating each other without respect to gender or rank, appearing as if they were total, ridiculing their own complexity, dispossessed of the present. A salamander joins the inspection, an act of surcease, compression, euphonious para-meditation, preventing the neutrality of an ovarian sun to endure in the matrix of taste from another identity's expectorant. Embalmed in the gravity of an icon, I coincide with the ethereal career of a spliced certainty considered without proportion, an induction ceremony always retreating into the repertory of loyal and impartial evasion, a continuity last played upon the parallel vitalities of the Before-the-Became and the analogion, unbearable exactitude causality officiates as a homeomorphic isonomy, lain at the door of Cercylas with an officer's laurels, the seizure of all rapine and defiled reports, evidence of the matter taken into the thousand hands attempting beatitude as a sacrifice to the throne, seen and never truly alone.

Io: Was this inviolate unit such a behemoth as it wandered What-It-Would-Be-Like, its pro-state emissions prostrating Without-and-To-Make?

Dr. Tiresias: I agree. A one-dimensional number line is a mighty and stimulating stage for a permanent revolution.

Adam: I AM.

Dr. Tiresias: Don't be rash unless you can rationalize it.

A divinatory flame embellishes the virgin gold spraying out across the old formula of appearance, the same times and merging eyes of systatic tanget space, omni-directional sockets gripped by bare nerves of siloxane, rotating tendrils of toothed, transparent lace-light in resplendent and mute equipollence.

Adam: I am the force of those who are out again, the exercise in Oxyrhynchus therapy tabulating a tunnel fanned with residual vacancy and liminal Diadochi biomes, the probes of entire judicial syncretisms of the *Strategos Autokrator*, bedecked with leonine robes and a leopard's skull.

[*The podium struggles to regain the air as its position at the pinnacle of the forum refinishes itself in normed vector space, nowhere to be seen. The impression that all of this has happened before and will awaken from its sleep to its death continues to reoccur until it is finally deployed, a miracle in the improbable belief. The basics of* No-Way-In: *an illiterate arabesque thrown around denuded normality humor graduating to ash in the deserted vapors of playback.*]

Gen. Hating: I am your escort.

Io: And I am your consort, a tall drink of water with legs like nuclear redundancy.

Dr. Tiresias: That would seem the best retention you've offered.

Io: From within, but from without . . .

Dr. Tiresias: We are all where we belong, in a decomposing raiment that pleases the sensors.

Io: So the *editio princeps* informs us.

Dr. Tiresias: We are an expeditionary force demanding the formal language of skepticism.

Io: Suppliants singing our bondage to the vector monitor freely.

Dr. Tiresias: I am the perpetrator of the At-Least-I-Am acquisition format.

Io: An estimable commemoration of our father-figure's omphalos syndrome.

Dr. Tiresias: Infinite and infinitely close to zero. A public address to redress the public for addressing itself in public: the hyper-meridian we use to justify our mediocre superiority and other inevitable paradoxes, for all the youth of the Marianas Trench whose brains return smelling like monothalamea spawned in an unused viaduct. Then we are done, microbial asterisms of watery dandruff, rejected even by gravitational collapse; brave, destitute, with cheeks like a skein of mesothelioma overlaying a thin sheet of ancient terracotta.

Io: *Karl Marx the Spot,* the title of the recital. The title of the piece to be recited: *The Dawn Breaks/Her Vested Interests.* The title of the hour it is to be performed: *The Sun Shakes/Her Dwindling Wedlock.* The title of the place it is to be recited: *She Goes/An Ostracized Strobe Light in Her Shapeless Porphyry.* The title of the hour after the recital: *Cheap Trinkets/Never Get to Very Much.* The title of the hour before the recital: *Faceless Brother or Faceless Sister/ Voiceless as the Sun.* The title of the audience: *No Longer Shall We Accept the Light/In Absence of the Mother Liquor.* The title of myself as I deliver the recital: *The Moon Is but the Icing On the Frieze/We Should Roll It Out of the Sky/To Use As A Magnifying Glass/Against Our Allies.*

Gen. Hating: At the Solatarium on Luna.

Io: In a fallow arbor of endomorphic time.

Dr. Tiresias: The educational parks where white dwarfs and quark stars are ejected in a mist finer than a wave of light receding in a stellar remnant.

Gen. Hating: Where we review the silk worms under the pretense of motion.

Adam: These events attract the epsilon-delta definition of limit embedded in the Total Titan's focus. Be we baleful, wise, vainglorious in the eyes of Heliogabalus or Ashurbanipal, Augustus or Sargon, who invoke the penance of immortality.

Dr. Tiresias: To speak the truth gives the illusion of freedom.

Io: That's just what we need to believe.

I reproach my compatriots for not having educed, yet wise in dexterity they excite the glory of having none other than wisdom to excite. Their rhetoric is endless.

5

THE
PLUTO
PROTOCOL

The first law of silence is to remain unperceived. This communication occurs in the neon gardens of Lucullus, the black boughs of the dead moriai like webs of charred bone hung with the depleted, oscillating ghosts of yesterday's fading animation, the flickering specters of broadcast vapor snagged like transparent silk shrouds on these ossified nerves of exposed bituminous fantasy, aspiring their last thin digital whisper of outdated programming: the twitching glee of obsolescence: *sub specie aeterni causa sui.* The rivers of the underworld are here collected: Cocytus, Phlegathon, Styx, Acheron and Lethe. *Monstrum in fronto, monstrum in animo. Why seek to teach me I have nothing to learn? What falsehood is the greatest student? He cannot wear his signal without his cipher: he cannot oblige himself to be anyone without first letting them know.*

REVISION (ATTEMPT):

Phlegathon: I am Phlegathon, the one who made the mistake that won't return.

Lethe: I am Lethe. You know what they say: if we all do as little as possible, we can.

The gravel burns against the image of their evil eyelashes, the red and white blood cells clenching a deteriorated war film of stolen munitions, the intestines of alien warships, yellow and mildewing goat's brains churning in vats of spectroscopic imaging serum. *If they want spies in their spider web, let them sate themselves.* It is time to harvest the radiation. A flaming satellite peeps through a window of sky on its trajectory towards this pit-planet of purple andesite, Gordian colossi, and the black phosphorous bled from human lips.

ENGINEERING:

Lethe: I am Lethe, always. When I have been reinstated, as I have graduated my mirror, I am the most potent parasite of the simulacra.

Acheron: I am Acheron. If I want to hear you, speak softly, so fancifully I will convey a verifiable certificate containing an updated and inauthentic curse.

Lethe: I am Lethe, the product of a million unnatural births. I have as much right to destroy more than what we are as you.

Acheron: I am Acheron, in all places and times. This must be you having the power to wield reality again.

The army in the distance a pale shadowy blur, they extend toward the placenta of the mountains, where it is extinguished. The peasant officers arrayed in asphodels recite their X-Ray purified refrains. Comparative necro-scions bask with their pellucid bovine. *I have no idea which one I am. Which one is he?* they ask. *Certainly not that one.* None. We and they each contain the capacity for both nobility and depravity. *I have found their presence an outrage against the purple garden's description, though I cannot describe the description.*

INHIBITION:

Acheron: I am Acheron, siren of the flash and bray. Balloons of monstrous flesh and igneous shards of confetti fall like fruit in the dark. The applause contracts. The ultra-violet luminosity of chaos.

Cocytus: I am Cocytus, my horn gives restraint to my allegiance.

Acheron: I am Acheron. Despair.

Cocytus: I am Cocytus, the dreaded. Everything is a component of the common nature.

Acheron: I am Acheron, the triumphant depletion. Everything is a component of the personal.

Cocytus: I am Cocytus. Against this I commit the Law.

Acheron: I am Acheron. Against this I commit Hysteria.

Cocytus: Tongues. I am Cocytus. I am the position that de- and en- thrones.

Acheron: I am Acheron, the aromatic weakness, simple dreams promote my plague.

Cocytus: These are my materials for exploitation. I am Cocytus. Reality is always dreaming.

In the deafening rush of shades the throne pursues a stone inamorata. The stage is illegible. *Reality is demeaning,* a sour thrush transcribes on a bucolic star: *No one is meant to be forgiving.* All the maneuvers of the disappearance that never occur, disembodied gestures crying out in the silence of guilt and honor never observed. Every species of lifeless horror accumulates, every vacant atrocity, every atonal violation of unspeakable ritual. The edges switch off. The caste once was. The court argues the severed force of those it educates. Strange purple stars for all, in the passive calderas of the sumptuous purge, where myself and my subjects persist, the judge forthcoming, behaving as if the Law were here trembling in a convex mirror of meteoric glass, a secret message of stillborn, conscious, and alien light squirming remotely in a dark crystalline grape the size of a human head. *I tell him there is no need. We are all opposed to everything we can think of; there is no need to know what those things are. Let us eat cake.* A cake decocted from spoiled polonium, agate of phlox and spurious hellebore is brought in, held aloft by the disembodied heads of a hundred panthers. It looks forlorn, crestfallen, without waste, as if it misspoke to its maker and will never again possess a horoscope. Germane. Grievous. I simply cannot touch it. It is filled with the tears of the massive and inutile phenomena propagating the universe. Today is no holiday, no fortune for embellishment for the patrician's league, no supple Orithyia will burst forth spiraled in a vitreous latticello that glows under her skin, proclaiming the depth of the tidal ink encrypted in her genetic lacunae. The night must continue its operation, its enveloping sorcery, beleaguered by every wish.

Cocytus: I confess the establishment fascinates me. I am Cocytus, who will never confess where there is sleep.

Styx: The void is unbridled potential.

Cocytus: So it is with the offspring of nothingness. I am Cocytus, I have not slept.

THE PLUTO PROTOCOL

Styx: There is always sleep where one finds it.

Cocytus: Repeat.

Styx: You sleep where one imagines they find it. I am Styx, the flashing membrane of filial darkness, the vein of a phosphene detached from a star. I am the first to be perceived a nemesis.

Cocytus: I am angel Cocytus, belabored by the anamorphosis of a world unseen.

Styx: Your female manhood. I am Styx, the venom-bound of subterranean surfaces.

Cocytus: I am Cocytus. Our Gods have been ripped from their stars. They are here now, crossing our dungeon. We are the derangement of their impotent tears.

Styx: Their ankles smoothed from snake bites, they wonder how they found their former realm so appalling. They tell us what the night says. I am Styx.

Cocytus: Even the rivers are their animals. I am Cocytus, the doom of repression and individuality.

Styx: I am Styx, the flower that pretends to be all others.

Cocytus: And so I am Cocytus, brute lilies of the field and beast.

Styx: Our Gods are waiting to reclaim their shadows, to darken them against the light of their bodies, to grow then darker with them; our Gods are not Gods, they are merely those who named us. I am Styx, and I believe Nothing can be learned, so nothing must be taught.

ASYLUM

The stereographic projection of a de-natured feline admitted as a neurological form constant in the Even House's ashen facial diaspora. To provide a reproduction of the sanctuary of forgiveness, cobalt-tipped orange nerve tendrils dismember everything they believe to lack sincere criminality. The words *this is the way to my boutique* reverberate in their limitless address outside dimension. *If you cannot pay your debt, a eulogy is preferred to an epigram,* they say to those destined to meet in the professional schemata of a health pension drinking from a cup of poison. A lavender cortege in the electricity of amplified and penurious elevation hyperduces a systematized gentry-person with Byzantine distemper and a three-months-post-due ash-selective orphanage before assignation is complete. *You are free to complain as long as you reject the sympathies and the handouts betokening the office.*

Plutocracy awaits its gangrene of basalt, embowered by the numb salon that appears in the guile of permissive eugenics. The intentions to speak through a reverie speak through a revelry. Lesser initiates, it has been divulged, are here, after all, for eternity. In the logic of their tithe they squeal before meager apostasies, the thought that nothing is meager here turning them to think that everything is nothing. These underlings bestow the delicacy of their erosion, their uniformity demanding decay, the clairaudient administrative *nomenklatura* that privileges the depraved as well as those they've defiled with invention in halls more spacious than the shackles of haste, where yellow cake is served and those they call *themselves* with inch long purple orca devour pieces of sutures bereft of wounds, all while removing their pariah's eyes from crazed control-mine children who must dine on their own magnetic scars. These weapons revert to their female limbs, the steel triggers of their wards fossil encrusted gimlets of demand, coils of ossified leeches their countenance: two distinct organisms sharing a single molecule. They kick without legs, the hermetic heresies of nameless Echo dressed as nubile and bellowing as the bruise-colored Oreads of Pluto, where the Boeotian craters detain the vacant still-houred lesser constructs of fledgling narcissists fallen from the dead bower nest of their mother's hope, their stamens purposeless and excrucied screaming, *Keep away, my lover! Keep away, my life-love!*, she responds, licentiousness searing her cheeks to a violet emanation of the scarlatina, her tongue smacking between her lips as if they were the lids of a lizard's eye. The suddenness of an unseen authority suspends her inversion, a trickling neurasthenia whispers its way through the cavity of her chest. A wish to be more mute than a moan departs with the revelation of what should be: an iris that separates like the gentle contusion of a mouth drawn vertically.

This planet is a brothel where the darkness is offered as a body, where rights are touched and changed into echoes. The smell of death loves the smell of muscle. What raptor unconsciously swells gazing back without warning into the eyes of swimming flame? Now we are desperate to crystallize. *You have tried to be a good structure, are you trying now to fail?*

A dishonored whisper kissing the feeble vortex of a sea-sponge, letting in unknown fury:

—*We have been banished from this side of infinity to the other. Do you think the universe has worth, or do you feel there is nothing sacred left in this wombless world?*

—*There is certainly nothing to protest.*

—*One tears open the nuptial: one wouldn't dare too much to ask.*

—Take your issues up with those who pay your taxes: I've assented to my assets.

—You are the superior, thus most accessible, if fame belies dejection.

—What are we?

—Carousing in a place where we must remain in chains.

—Eleutheria.

—Entopticon.

—Like us.

The ultimate magnitude of division ascertained, the deformed parallelism of sub-conscious matter attends to the banquet. People of an alien race: this is what makes them taste correctly or incorrectly. All Martians taste like cosines: *that is correct.* All Mercurians believe purple onions taste like a midwife. That, too, is correct, when vanquished in the ultra-violet oubliette of a perpetual radio midnight, yet incorrect at midday, when onions taste like metamorphic sine waves in the dark underbelly of an O-Negative lagoon. All those born on Jupiter believe water tastes like a plain of sulfur: barren. This is incorrect. Water tastes like an epicenter for phenomena who have never tasted anything, having been fed their entire life intravenously. Now, if a member of the epicene species mewling about a forensic race assumes the terrain is remote, perfidious, without lode, stellar table, or chart, a clepsydra for when they join their exterior gender to calcium, proffering not a scrape or a scab, they must then be dialogical.

On the subject of Space, which is the only subject, we must now consider tribal factionalism with all participants who maintain a corresponding fetish for the material. The Babylonians, for instance, who inculcated a dietary poverty when it came to infant mortality rates, have found a practical tantalization in considering infinite mortality rates, which has increased infant immortality rates, as well as the production of abnormal ecstasy in offspring without origins, or Aborigines. This has been the true goal of their exercise. All predominating masculine attributes have aligned, shedding their identities in an isometric projection of cis-Ethos, a faculty of erroneously simulated trans-Bathos, distilled from the surreal numbers, stellar remnants, and other illusive internal properties of artisanal yellow cake. The purple cyclosilicate darkness opens like a closet door in the unborn atmosphere enshrining the non-product, allowing featureless hybrids of mold-mothers to step like clay onto the degraded elder soil, with no choice but to return all prayers to the boiled hairless flesh baking upon their bones in the charred obsidian light as it retreats from their bodies back to the skeletal halo of an empty neutron star, a spheroid oven removed from proportion, presenting each member of its theosophy treadmill with equality of sanitization.

A shard of glass retrieves a stalactite, a most auspicious peregrination, Eurydice remarks. *It aims at my throat. Let it synchronize and sink in . . .*

Black snow coughs from a gash in the purple magma. The shades at our feet huddle closer. The chasm that is my palace stares back into me, down the iridescent black robes that drape my body. My reflection is my queen. I meet her with a gaze of purple sapphire; she is not a woman who could love me; I am as I am not. The black Orpheus desecrating his Persephone with a lavender strain. A gust of wind from my throat fans the cryptobiotic terrarium of the black desert, a fading tunic of light limping over it, exiting to Taenarum with the sound of ascendant legs: beautiful, strong, carved, lissome and robust, rising into the lichen flames the guests and slaves alike wear as skirts. They have been released, they assure me. An enormity overwhelms the air. The mongrels stampede over their prey, after-cheering the decay they leave, the expanse of my wound like a hollow murmur incinerate, the great apse of my lungs mandated from Tyrian ink, expanding and retracing each impossible invocation. Persephone as Eurydice vanishes from my sight. The prisoners clutch their eyes, a reception conflagrating and blind. They clutch the ears of the pit till they are deafened by it; thus they vanish with the chill of their fingerprints upon the black soil where grow, somewhere like skin over the darkening laughter, the echoes of insects preparing to descend, the echos engorged upon each other, the senses as purple as the snow filling the bags of skin where our veins have evaporated.

6

IO,
THE BIONIC VENUS

Today is the Gift of Baiae. I'm in my motorcycle leather, the golden ringlets of my hair compressed in the helmet. Everything has been assembled. The target: Astro Incitatus, a Russian "vacation" broker. To the victor go the spoils.

I am as closed as an eye, the leather perforated by silver spikes, each spike engraved with the image of an imperial suicide standing erect in the same suit of spiked leather, thus: Astro Incitatus, like an oil slick risen to the state of Man. He holds out three fingers, then runs one across his neck. A plume of green smoke rises behind him emanating the stench of the inferno: sulfur, melting glass. The flames gorge themselves on the pyre of the temple. Three vestals scream. This reminds me of a nameless girl in Latvia, who was being rented to one Augustus Circus Maximus. She looked like a little boy beaten to death when I found her. In the name of the Father of Our Country and God I remedied this mistake. They found a picture of Augustus on the toilet, his contribution to the human race mutilated: they never found him. I am having him drained at the moment.

Astro Incitatus has spread his face through all digital media like a smeared cartoon whose frozen upper lip catches on one cell in the frame and drags across every other, never dissolving. He kicks his MT-10 into gear as a pavonine flame bursts through the temple gate, the dome buckles, collapses. The screams cease. Those who fall victim before me do so only because they were impossible to save. An ascendant eagle spreads its wings out of the flames leaving a trail of red smoke to dry to a nervine stain across the sky. Now I look for my enemy who has departed, the puddles of rain split like petals and cress leaves behind him. The first time will be the last. The odor of a language secreted by unknown and inexhaustible terrors follows him on his incline towards maximum atrocity. I have identified myself as the operator who will redact the phenomena of his life. The eagle expands in an ethylic mist across what never was, the embodiment of this hyperplane plague, the last for humankind.

The stage is a thousand jewel-encrusted man-o-war linked. The water is a single phosphene multiplying the shimmering waves of its mirage by graph points out across a directionless face. This is the greatest Hell Heaven has to offer. I descry my pursuers through the cavalcade. Astro Incitatus has buried both young and old, beautiful and homely, decadent and penniless, equally in rich black earth and ashes. With each compression he believes he proves that all mortals receive what they confess in their hovels, into fissures in the marble of their palaces, their pleas carried on spider eggs to the cribs where their inheritors aspirate long dry goads sucking in the polyp tincture of tainted Time, the whittled ghost of venom, to be punished for perfection and imperfection alike. That is how he develops: the foot sinks down on the lever to shift, the femur cracks, the ribs crack, the spine and the neck align, the blood wells through the lacerated pavement, the dark radius of the pool palpable as a man who is his own agenda personified. *We with bodies are privileged to relinquish them,* the worms subscribe the cave crickets to their pedagogy of doom, clothed in their festering shells:

Just as every work of caution demands a silent and permanent devastation of unspeakable serenity, the temptation to debride an individual with the power of your gender directs its magnitude. Those with nominal finances find themselves presented as lesser properties: the man with the fewest wives to extort has the fewest slaves. Good or Evil, Good AND Evil, accord the experiences they themselves are too shallow to substantiate, warranting less than no comment. Those with unlimited resources are thus afforded what they can afford: unlimited opportunities to exploit their unlimited opportunities, opportunities befitting their ineluctable altitude and mystique. Grandeur and prowess are the requisites of such a station. Is this why we must blind ourselves to the woes of both overseer and bottom feeder to serve with integrity those whose fortunes are rarefied labyrinths ending in the exquisite horror of the entire populace? This is an archaic theorem disproved before it was educed. We must blind ourselves in order to see ourselves blind. We must blind ourselves to see ourselves as we truly are, negotiated out of our flesh by the charlatans of Fortune whose blindness went without witness.

The burning purple water of the Bay of Baiae receding in a digital simulacrum of reality behind, every thirty seconds the voice recites a new ideal: *You can foster blame for those who attain immortality, but not for their unethical conduct. Through no fault of their own they live without consequences, requisitioning the ideal, obliterating the bitter contemptuous wicked stares that guide their frivolity to dramatic accesses of elation, a tempest of tears and tart bodily fluids, irreducible provocations swallowed by a crowd of dreams. This is the geneaology of all that has been said.*

From the parapet Astro Incitatus projects his presence over the orator's in a dark blanket of nano-mares, a fleet of bacterial robots carrying in fractal reduction his patho-logical imprint, a panther's roar consuming the speaker, a transfusion of poisoned vitality, gorged embolisms flayed across every flawed node of this incorrect, manacled, gulf-drown corpse-parabola of Time. The villain approaches the primordial elution. He speaks: *To understand where we are our people must seek the justice of the atrocities they jealously guard, for we are the children of a jealous God, and I am very interested in denying you justice. I am the associate of swept-away thistle, a satin caiman devoid of emotion yet emotive, a Cossack constrictor, in a word: the most interesting luminary to ratchet a fledgling's neck. I am a male, voted most likely to mount a pythoness. If you are a female, you have been elected to my overseas' fortress, where you cannot afford to live. Here you will receive trans-panoplianism, which you have volunteered for, according to your couch, as put forth in Section X, Paragraph 3, Subsection V of last week's episode. As for the worshipers of Hermaphroditus, I have no money to lend you. Please shoulder your infantilist burden until you can be replicated, reprogrammed and replaced. All epicene spices have been purchased, imbibed, digested and expelled. For this we give you half-price, a circumstance that will help provide our enemies the right impression of our contemporary society, one they are not important enough to live in. The best they can hope for is a marginal slot in the race-war simulator for twenty minute clerks inattentive as stillborns. Who's watching nobody in the para-forensic ethernaut laboratory? Old man, must you transvestite yourself at every adopt-a-border? The stage is infected with the products of our ancestors. We follow them with their own eyes to their dressing rooms where they take off their bandages and mirrors, prancing around dressed in only their keyholes: this is what my associates and I are willing to do for you. Anyone seen fit to provide us citizenship (a piece of furniture in the badlands) is asking us to live in a cage (utilities included) until our feet are only a part of us, as we remember. Putrefy the purchase! If you detect our bones through our blisters they must be leaking dietary enzymes and triglycerides, a fragrance of fruit dissolved in acetic acid, timeless abrasions turned to vermillion-green tortoises crushed against the clouds where the collapsing sun is distilled into a phantasm of oil, lime flower water, an amphibious moss erupting in a whorl of pellucid reptile eggs and white berries only our lingering hate can devour. There is no call for concern: you've already lost more than we could ever gain from you.* In the depths of his clarity Astro Incitatus extols his injury.

My helmet off, my golden tresses longer than light, incandescent strands scented to resemble quicksand, perfidy. I don't trust them, though I love them. *They* don't trust *me*. In the illusory bastion of my offense, the summer, querulous as a demigod, walks on stilts over the water, the acetic ether of sunset flaring, the voice of caution a dull one indeed. This is the gymnasium of evolution: Astro Incitatus presents the President his pen. With a click our only interest is the gas flooding our mouths, the mannerisms we adopt to escape it, the water shaved tension slivered by injected bodies to tongue tips. *You'll never leave your suzerainty.*

Astro Incitatus floats in grandeur through the melee, the sunken throats expostulating, their hands cropped without rank, having failed to claw the surface they sought. No proposals of signs in the ovarian swelter, the only thing the exposed day has left to offer. Io, the signatory of the hour's sepulcher. Astro Incitatus, deranged by his own spectacle, dips into a prison to dispense with the moment of truth, addressing himself as if he were his own mother relieved to see him in his frequent skin, stalling the future to remain in this moment of majestic pretension and anointment. *There's no way back to where we're going; there's no way out of where we've been.*

Discord from here to there, insatiable, apprehending the pseudo-not. Two voices free of themselves mimic each other. Two voices, two helpless creatures buried in ester who can't tell the difference between one's thoughts and the struggle in the other's throat. Two voices magnificently crazed and dissipated. Two voices no one wants to hear yet the world obeys. The voices of opposing fountains. We are compelled to hear, under their seismic vat, where a lithium ion transposes the critical mass of a phoenix feather, boiling a froth of fabular tears, the final atom shaking with fear as it lays upon the cold voices of those who failed to revolt: they are all we care for, tiny wreathes of scum lining the gums of an Astro Incitatus newly erected in bronze. In a womb-like nexus of plaque, Trauma nods her assent.

Disorder paused in unbridled vibrancies, warped constitutions pulling into the fray shrivel, darkly luminous they handle the muscle with polished lunula. Without coercion Astro Incitatus, manic in his spurs, rears his black mane as if executing innumerable undesignated patrons of subterfuge halfway between two countries that span planets, the body of water that is his mouth encompassed by a desert. He calls us from the shore, turning to glass the sky above, a universe of regulations contrived by rulers we cannot comprehend. *What is the name of the country where we are now rulers?* a certain voice asks aloud, surely not like this. Preening Astro Incitatus vibrates in reply a name I cannot repeat, his neck forced proudly, the plume of a quantity of fire. *All civilizations, all cultures, all countries, are guided by the same principal: deformity must be* abolished; if not abolished, worshiped. *Console your dead with this knowledge.*

To combat existential fraud, we must invent a crisis.

A vestal virgin, exhausted by her birth name, has escaped us. Her fellow priestesses call her The Squid to account for the unnatural tendrils that hang down from her shoulders and the bulbs that dangle from these. Her obscene limbs enwrapping the neck of Astro Incitatus as if she were his familiar. They cannot be wrenched from each other's grasp. *Don't listen!* she pleads. *The way you look is not as important as what's inside!*

The way you look is what's inside, we retort in every degree. Astro Incitatus, the leviathan formidable to the center of every moment, righteousness and savagery inextricable: *Christen her with a bacteria of lead and mercury, we shall see how beautiful her molten steam.* The other two virgins begin to work and laugh.

Inviolate, are we? I ask the more resonant of the pair, a smug pug-nosed blonde idolater with iridescent fingernails she would scrape across my face to renew her ingestion of blood. The decree stirs panic, immeasurable in the common face. This must be how untainted harlots ache to rescind their experiments. The flesh is a chain webbed in sterling and elastic vessel patterns, the harried stock footage of ever-facile propagation made vicious through the dynamism of contempt. The blonde's face a wad dripping her features down a smooth crimson coil wound in platinum filaments, netted are her pleas with it, soughing madly her bosom, her touch petrifies the arid field of vision around her, an instant expressed as a crop. No motive to desire her words' maturation now. An influx of frequencies and Astro Incitatus assures his fanatics, an insolvent tribunal of flames matted against the sky:

The blood has finally reached the trial, frenzied, in triplicate, but also slender, cloven like a cat's iris, a stroke of compulsory health. The city whimpers bemusedly, a patent leather vulture tears one organ after another out of their desolates wells, rending every nation perceived, every tender hush of misfortune. The pursued pull back to breathe, their lucidity abates, inside. They marvel at Astro Incitatus, his genius, his classified demeanor, his memory a bay of counterpoised methodologies sluicing against a deserted mirror. Incitatus is well, he pronounces over the whole affair. He remains a version of himself amused by his extremities, the crippling mass of power wielded by his arms, his legs like cannons, his head a cannonball with the function to smite dimensions with every promise. Human dignity will not entreat him. He has no behavior. No matter how bizarre, he has long since attained the timbre of the supra-infra-observable; his splendors, crowded and leering, witness his entreaties and ordeals. Not one of them has been dishonored or announced. Mutilated and gargantuan, they prevail upon the shapes of their after-rights.

Dismounting, Astro Incitatus takes Io by the leg. The remainder of a vestal virgin—for she is—and as such, leaps onto the back of Astro Incitatus, stabbing his spine with a laser. A foaming rostrum spews to her. A provisional throng stirs an oration: *No one deserves the right! For those in power, it only impedes the force necessary to govern; for the governed, it serves solely to promulgate an ideal they can never attain. In this salacious world of virtuosic luxury, men and women are beneath each other, conveyed to their gorgeous oblivions by celibate vegetables and celebrity tiger-toyers. That is why we all must be preemptively scrutinized, convicted, and punished. If you would like to leave a message, leave it in our mouths then listen through our ears like a million seashelled beach for a reply!* It is someone's duty to extort this argument, the encountered problem dealt in every notion, the constant externalization of repetition, premiering against the natural authority of the highest objects we are said to have been possessed of at birth. Clarified: one can give or take what is needed.

Even in the popular word *renaissance* what-does-not-have-to-be is privileged to take place. Astro Incitatus kills me, for I am his partner. I have the right to remain silent: it can never be taken away.

We can't stop men from telling us how to look or act so we make them our husbands, flaunt them, encapsulate them, oppress them by withholding what they want most. At last we abolish their virility by denying them access to even their pettiest scandals. This is our PRAXIS, oversimplified for sophisticated pedestrians, unformed minds with uniform vices: the humility of the superior: all expressions of violence abolished by subtlety. These are the thoughts of a beautiful woman when the night has come too late and too dark.

Primogeniture concepts directed by incongruity make earthly statements reliant on the future. Astro Incitatus is prepared to schism. The blast of my ordnance delivers upon my nemesis such force it sends the vestal virgins skipping like three dark stones across the sea, back to no other shore, for I am his assassin.

7

DREAM SYSTEMS

A dim sad boy alone in the reliquary of his cereal and the angel light of his softly breathing Saturday morning cartoons. His mother has just died and his father he has never known. In a moment of unutterable loss, the social worker will take him to the foster home. For now, not thinking of his family or of himself, thinking of nothing else, he aerates his sadness with the autonomous movement of nonlife on the screen as if consumed by the mesmeric waves of a baetylus:

Inter-dimensional tycoon Vorpal Montetiavore, his nephew Oximaldor Montetiavore, Oximaldor's son Maltetiavore Montetiavore, as well as their dog, Huxtamoine-Valterpimonte Montetiavore, are seeking to contact Vladislav Surkov in the Atlas Mountains, yet somehow they've ended up in the Andes. "He's a very famous science fiction writer, from what I've heard," asserts Maltetiavore Montetiavore when asked by his grand-uncle who they are searching for, why they are searching for him, and what they are going to do when they get there.

"We're going to ask him to write our story and if he doesn't we're going to sue him," answers Oximaldor, at the moment obviously a lawyer.

"Reality is not important in this context," Vorpal assures everyone, "but I recall reading somewhere that the man we're searching for has the computing power of a tau particle, three quarters of a gluon, and half the Z bosons in a time machine."

"Is that supposed to be a lot?"

"If it is, I'm going to offer him some money."

"And what if he already has some?"

"I won't offer him very much."

"We always have this same conversation every time we're here."

They've arrived. "You are the product of your cis-credit," a compulsory voice warns them. A remonstrating mother materializes through the ubiquitous, prepared in a freeze frame. Jiang Qing, accompanied by a poisoned assignation, panegyrizes: "Mama is home from a hard days work. Our debts have accumulated like unfulfilled wishes, stale and drown in worm castings. They've prepared a film to explain the process: monotone flowers, nameless insects, and other tropical guests on the screen. A ceaseless shape-shifting that is unstoppable because it is undefinable. All that appears is good: whatever is good will appear."

The sky above a transparent sheet of deoxidized amino acid, the Montetiavore clade disaffected. The nephew speaks: "Things will go darkly as darkly they enter, from here till then." The grand-nephew: "The promise of fun was the fun of the promise."

A projection of a mannequin's unallotted face: Science has been evacuated: flat unmentionable emulsion. The mother: "You'll see and you'll stay in what you see, listening to the flattering threnody of the paused place, becoming what they listen to, as, darkening, the old things take on new visages and stay where they are. We've all had it happening: looking half at yourself, a partial constriction of the constructed place, soundless ruin running down the empty barrel of a finger. Very much, for years. The key to sustaining friendships with unknowable relations that loss will make important is the places you don't look, the everlasting passing."

Vorpal Montetiavore: This proves that excessive flattery can lead to the accomplishment of only certain goals.

Maltetiavore Montetiavore: We've each entered the scene with two bodies, yet none of us is the King of Nature.

Oximaldor Montetiavore: I, myself, am in a two person body, and this woman is doubtlessly a Cleopatra Caesar, manipulating her body against inferior beings for their own sake.

Vorpal: Once more you prove yourself the author of substandard protocols, standard procedures, and standardized social formulae.

Oximaldor: The semantic web of an anti-natalist.

Jiang Qing produces a small lunar sun from an invisible demarcation: "This is the *Mater Idaea Deum*. Soon its benignant seeds will crowd the sparrows balanced on their stalks of grain, the finches and wrens and nascent flamingos, like a maze full of extra-sensory shallots."

"A spectacular critique of the spectacle," says Oximaldor, patting Huxtamoine-Valterpimonte's head and speaking in a combination of Sumerian and Greek so the dog, too, can understand. The oven of the windless present turns away from its vegetation. Apoptosis. Proxy-colors and the hyper-real numbers of interoperability. Automated engineering. Strange stars. The anodyne boy conducting this dot matrix data structure through the glowing green aura of his personal chromosphere a destabilized image, a destabilized perception.

Vorpal Montetiavore picks a skeleton from a pill bottle then washes it down with a three day's hydrogen ration. A female figure whose body is a pocket of light appears, one of the Corona Gemini. She rears her gaze of intransigent radiance out across the forming night, abolishing it with her resplendence.

Jiang Qing: That was her one chance and she overacted. Suffocating.

Oximaldor: It was lovely while we were having dinner; unfortunately, she misapprehended her own pluck.

Jiang Qing: The strain of her decorative prayers makes it not worth knowing who she is.

Oximaldor: *How do you eat?* she asks me.

Vorpal: Every gratuity devolving from satisfaction ...

Oximaldor: Where was the element of carnage? Should she involve herself in a response ...

Vorpal: Who knew we were expecting her ...

Maltetiavore: I don't know who I am, but I would like to know what's for dinner. (*He falls into a secondary asepsis on the verge of oraculating.*)

Jiang Qing: Now the silver is embarrassed.

Oximaldor: A bastard child is a lying child.

Jiang Qing: Fortunately you're not only his father, but his mother as well.

Oximaldor: Aren't you glad to be disoriented to hear the familial overtones of your effusions vying with each other like data object class relationship properties?

Maltetiavore: Maybe I should watch the news while I exude an exterior calm ...

Oximaldor: An assignation begins to eat.

Jiang Qing: An important life is the essence of concision.

Vladislav Surkov beams down from a spaceship: Don't call me Vlad the Inhaler or any of that reframing the narrative filth. I'm looking for an impudently selfish bastard child to marry my mother.

Oximaldor: Selfish and distinguished, that would be me.

Vladislav: So I hear you've been paying someone to dream of my mother?

Oximaldor: I am a dream in which language assigns itself its symbols.

Maltetiavore: He is an instrument similar to thinking.

Oximaldor: I am the Not-Thinking-of-Anything-Thought, if you prefer.

Jiang Qing: What I wouldn't give to have a preference for mare's milk.

Vorpal: There are accomplishments that look better on paper in crystal.

Jiang Qing (*disgorging a bent systrace onto a plateau*): Let the boy eat or I am going to eat the boy!

Vladislav: You're too eager to position the future, mercenary beast.

The Lothario Brigade arrives from Turkey, along with The League of Byzantine Postivists, deploying from hang-gliders into their individual cages, untouched by the perimeters of the sky and the jaws of the Earth functioning as mountain ranges. Simultaneously they retract their hands and join them. In the distance, Turkey grows to the size of its own continent, producing a third of the world's sterilized amoebas and repurposed windshield sticker adhesive, saving the first two dimensions from annihilation.

Jiang Qing: The grace of the bastard child stretches through the eye-hole in camelopardalis. With one hand we salute, with the other we struggle to hold the blade.

Malteteiavore: Let us squirm in a facsimile of defiance until the zeptosecond in command arrives.

Jiang Qing: This is the time for women dressed like me. (*She clamors through a door in a rocky precipice, catching hold of her own hair in the darkness. Her wrists shrink and her forearms bulge. She cries while not crying at all.*)

What is wrong with this sad lady? thinks the boy, his life now some faraway promise that will never be fulfilled.

"What is this supposed to demonstrate?" asks Oximaldor Montetiavore.

"An auspicious form of self-awareness," responds Vladislav Surkov with constructive ambiguity.

"The table is cleared," rejoins Jiang Qing, motioning to Malteiavore Montetiavore, who has allowed himself to bloat with hunger.

"I will acquiesce to the mood of my environment," he observes, harvesting the mistaken identities deteriorating in the throats of his companions into a bounty of immaterial pledges and halted supplications.

Vladislav: The documented means of usurping a former lover's inviolate deceit promote the ruin of the concubine's thievish offspring, as well as any social life derived from it.

Oximaldor: Actions worthy of, yet beyond, reproach.

Vladislav: This is what our grandmother's teach.

Jiang Qing: The sign as well as the signified have lost control of their relational database schema.

Vladislav: We must climb inside their emotions with a sling blade to see if an apoplectic evil is the right conclusion.

Jiang Qing: No one knows what evil is these days. It is our typical sacred duty to manner them into it.

Oximaldor: The result of hyper-normality.

Jiang Qing: I've come here to reject or be rejected.

Vladislav: You are only a guest. Execute yourself, as well as your rudimentary duties, as if composing a vaccine I could neither hate nor endure.

The sunset, a haze of green calcite covered by a lavender curtain and ringed in golden coils, strokes its many nameless harbors, gathering in the composite of its forms. Jiang Qing, soundless mother of Operation Optic Nerve, admits that she can only do so much with this family of entrancing miscreants who dance in and out of reality like liquid crystal dream lattices, half seen, half intuited.

Oximaldor: Clearly, spontaneous human combustion is an under-appreciated faculty similar to recreational clairvoyance.

Vorpal: When it happens or when it doesn't?

Jiang Qing (*rising abruptly*): So what if you can develop a photograph with domesticated E. Coli? What do the poultry think? What does their leader say?

Oximaldor: That it's twice as common as gold but eight times rarer than silver.

Valdislav: That an idiot staring out of a vacuum is a tedious substitute for vehemence.

Maltetiavore: Sink into a chair where at least your defeat will accept you.

Vladislav: I remember the featherless swans down at the automata interchange: there was never any need for them.

Oximaldor: As if there's ever a need for anything other than need.

Jiang Qing sees herself as an unwed mother washing her baby in a toilet: What is an idea capable of? Having been born without personhood, disguised as a master of disguise, I revisit such thoughts in the vespertine hours, when the husk of matutinal commotion parlays a vacant electron shell these people think of as a sun for a crippled moiety at the algorithm's bridge. We are standing in a room that will never finish itself, a guess-work of singular passions caretaking our shadows and our hollow, indeterminate lives. We are the consecrated brides articulating history for the pleasure of grace and damnation. Be with us as it is, Judea Pearl, with these images of need, the contemplated objects of *Homo Spectator*.

Maltetiavore: She's baked. Just excuse her and let us never falter in our fury and finesse of suppertime.

Oximaldor: Politely Bayesian, as he used to be. You can't imagine how sorry I am for it.

Maltetiavore: I would take me home with me, if I had been strangled at birth.

Jiang Qing: If the repast consents to be eaten, there is no reason to be jealous of it.

Vladislav: The agent's model of what you are will always be a cartoon, and in return you will see a cartoon version of the world through the agent's eyes.

Jiang Qing departs, signaling Larry Fink, who drops in from Black Rock or Black Water.

Vladilsav: If it isn't the consort's basileus.

Oximaldor: The neurophonic bitmap.

Maltetiavore: Suppers ruined.

Vorpal: As inadvisable as pragmatic parenting.

Larry Fink: Before I was born I appeared in many films, such as those that had come to their end, industrial grains in brittle celluloid like branches passing under the ice, long black hairs caught in the ghost of a waterfall falling upward, returning to its source. I recollect all these things as the mother of us all winterizes her lovers. What you have just seen wasn't a film: it was a battlefield with leisure as its weapon, the device accumulating so many maimed variants, so many hypotonic prodigies, mass social isolation and screen fatigue, non-linear warfare, the delicate balance of terror, the soul of the citizens like an unopened eye flickering on the crosswalk sign, simplified agents . . .

Oximaldor: The sign is the signified. Open it.

Larry Fink: I am as callous as that eye.

Oximaldor: It will never be clear who you are working for.

Larry Fink: Your name is Legion.

Oximaldor: Le-*sion.*

Maltetiavore: My name is Limp Lariat, because the lilac pudding is lame.

Jiang Qing (*re-entering*): Stunning. This meta-psychotic insect boy has eaten the sunset. Larry Fink, Jiang Qing. I know we're divorced, but I don't think we've been properly introduced.

Vladislav: That's right, rubberize your love till it screeches.

Larry Fink: We must ask ourselves, *Whose caricatures are we?*

Vladislav: I expect we should never question our circumstances.

Larry Fink: As Daniel Pearl, director of perception management for the Wall Street Journal, once told me, *Taking into account the condition of the human mind, an inhuman condition is preferred.*

Vladislav: The mind is an affiliate we must surrender our orders to in order to keep a compromising position without compromising ourselves.

Oximaldor: Ideal.

Maltetiavore: Prismatic.

Larry Fink: The ideals of the ones we love, if they don't conflict with our own ...

Vorpal: Premonitory doggerel that never should have rounded the square of escaping luck. Degenerate and burdensome.

Jiang Qing: I find it attractive, even if it is loathsome, like when the hierarchical order surrenders to its own facilities.

Larry Fink: For the sake of endangered husbands everywhere, we must dictate for pleasure alone.

Maltetiavore: Eating is too frequently wholesome.

Larry Fink: I am the arriving denouement.

Jiang Qing: Imminently victorious.

Vladislav: I feel as if I am suddenly a phantasmodean cross-current.

Into the reservoir of the image's electromagnetic aura the boy peers for the secret of the intermission. *Is it an experiment?* The science fiction historiography seems to have ended. *Was it a lament? Had he seen sympathetic characters being disassembled?*

He exists in a spool of microfilm, a 12-year-old partisan of an unknowable world created by the Lumière Brothers. We direct your attention to the saddest film ever produced, a masterpiece entitled *La Sortie de l'Usine Lumière à Lyon.* After it, the world will suffer the privilege of aging simultaneously forward and backward. The future and past confiscated, the present remains what it always was: a prison.

A bird of paradise manifests through the silent photosphere onto the screen, scampering over the surface of a serial number. Not knowing the meaning of the word *dispossessed,* the boy cries while not crying at all.

8

HORIZON: MARS

In ersatz *Spetsnaz* spacesuits, Io, the Bionic Venus, and Adam Tyrillion, codename: Trillions, circle a concentrated expression of the integrated spectacle, a commercial command structure identifying as substation *Omertà*, itself orbiting Mars, a pathogenic landscape plagiarized from the covers of countless sun-bleached science fiction novels, the confluence of innumerable mysteries, voyage deprived of its temporal aspects and its reality of space.

Adam: Terminal zenith achieved.

Io: The final denial of humanity.

Adam: The conspiracy theory of history has achieved its hypostatization. The demi-elite have achieved the apex of fundamental darkness: the erasure of personality.

Io: The universe reports for toponymic reprocessing. May every dormant decoy, every featureless and hollow object of ephemera and frivolity, every media particle accelerated to trans-light speed, inhabit their imaginary time.

Adam: *In a void without memory, images flow and merge like reflections on water, demanding to be heard in their soundless pleas for an unattainable discernment.*

Io: Compared to terrorism, anything is acceptable.

Adam: We wanted our nightmares to understand us. We found jealously guarded trivialities alluring simply because they evoked envy. Now reality is one substanceless catastrophe after another perpetuating themselves like nebulae of hollow, inaccessible light in the hypoxia of our perception.

Io: Science must remain subservient to profit. It is unacceptable to construct an industrial strategy on environmental imperatives or other illusions of pre-spectacular human experience.

Adam: Practical and analytical decadence, the inflation of devalued signs of life, hybrid warfare: where disinformation is named, it does not exist.

Io: You say it, then I say you said it, then you say it was I who said *this*.

Adam: Matter's condemnation of its own existence is a stage in its self-programmed destruction.

Io: That's what I was hoping you'd say.

Adam: You can say that, then I can say I regret you saying it, then you can say you regret all hope, I'll say that's regrettable, you'll say you'd hope, I'll say it feels like we're identical twins who share but a single gene, you'll say we're man and wife, I'll say I hope, and you'll say you regret.

Io: It is impossible to show that no one is laughing.

Adam: Say whatever you want, I'll say whatever I want, afterwards, when nothing has been said, we'll say how we said nothing, which is really something, then I'll say how you wanted to say what you neither wanted to say nor said, you'll riposte the same, and so the commodity contemplates itself in a world of its own constitution.

Io: I wouldn't say so, simply because you did. The evidence of this crime must be the lack of evidence. I can't stand it when robots speak robotically.

Adam: The enjoyment of transience is itself transient, just as war is a manifestation of *erotomania*, or the sickness of Eros. From the dominant science, or the science of domination, and other superior, more insubstantial forms of the American extermination clause, economists have discovered how much of the appearance of life an individual can maintain in their encounter with the eminently perceptible pseudo-event *death*.

Io: While you philosophize on the techniques of illicit confinement and circular data information as if they were the road-maps of universal history, your subsidized respiratory system has lived a period of three days, during which we have mated and had a family. After a disagreement involving one of your holograms, whom I denied having manipulated into crawling through the intestines of a defunct star cruiser then through a solar tunnel leading to a prison-pod, all appeared amicable, or at least relatively so. Our children—cyborg bats with human wings—resembled ancient salon-types equivocating amongst the nuclear clouds our species left behind on Mars, trading faces with one another. Every soul on the planet below is our kindred.

Adam: Don't taint the scientific modesty of your interpretations by interposing reckless historical judgments, though they appeal to my higher instincts, and there could be no nobler sacrifice. Perhaps this attests to my servile sentimentality, which trickles down in riverine streams of burning orange and yellow onto the parched surface of this planet's early exosphere to merge with the solar wind.

Io: That would be shocking. Why didn't you just tell me how you were going to tell me then refrain from doing so?

Adam: Don't be larcenous. If it exists, there is no need to talk about it. We've seen the last breath of the last movie-mother and her children spilling out across a holocaust of lies, where ineptitude commands universal respect and there is nothing to eat but the immaterial mucous membrane of mass hallucination.

Io: Your good looks will run away with your friends, leaving you only a surface-stratum without resonance, bereft of even the ossified mineral deposits of your crippling doubts.

Adam: And who will repay me?

Io: Every intelligence agency in the galaxy, if you first provide them with the substance of your fears and a sigh to prove your weakness.

Adam: The rancor of a man who pays his friends to abandon him will not go unclassified.

Io: Thus we commiserate, despite the ineptitude of our sympathies.

Adam: We do not propose what is desirable, nor preferable, we simply record what *is*. History and democracy entered the world at the same moment; their disappearance has also proved simultaneous. We wipe away our tears with our pity for all mankind. This will be our trial, repaying charade with charade, tempest with tempest. Each expository dalliance must inevitably remain brisk and concise.

Io: Just as all experts serve the state, every decent desert in this mitochondrial DNA super-conductor deserves an insular penitent to stand seared by the sun on a pillar of salt.

Psyop or biome lensing, the grapheme ADAM grows considerably through the display of incessant technological renewal, integration of state and economy, generalized secrecy, unanswerable lies, and an eternal present.

Io: The most useful expert is the one who can lie.

Adam: *Men resemble their time more than their fathers.* If I say this infuriates me, it arouses the allies of propaganda to perform a vague invasion, one whose only consequence is an everlasting possession, and whose success, or at least rumor of success, is guaranteed.

Io: I have a notion of the sweep, the grandeur and magnanimity of your alabaster physique as it turns to dust, desiccated by the electromagnetic spectrum through which every living being must pass, every object, and everything between.

Adam: I let you insult my intelligence with the universe's gamma motor as if you were the grand physionaut whose body contains all will and all thought, the imperial psychoarch, the absolute master of memories who generates not only the template for energy itself, but the impulse toward energy. Are you a lady, and I am nothing more than the steed from which you purport yourself to be matriarch of both all acceptable truth and the unconditional lie that acceptable truth truly is?

Io: We can insult one another, but never with the truth.

Adam: Autocratic autophagia. Does the courtroom of space belong to the judge, the jury, or the people?

Io: The accused and their representatives. They arouse the greatest furor.

The Other World Economic Forum suddenly materializes, an academic quorum populated by reverse anti-bodies with human heads, aquatic limbs, and equestrian mannerisms. They are all flapping their lips and snorting, each pregnant with a creature from an unknown species. Utilizing a miraculous, recently synthesized ontological web language, or OWL, they set about their birth pains. A choir of hermaphroditic indo-reptiles and neutered homunculi freshly rendered from star-paste arise from the quire of the transparent cathedral of Space, vanquishing all human doubt with their rapturous odes.

The Saturday Matinee Made-for-TV Movie begins:

Scene 1: A tower of sunlight: tanning in its rings of radiation: a lean, golden-haired, well-muscled he-man. Squirting noxious juices out of the pimples in his armpits, turning the entire desert to a trail of dust in the wake of his kevlar tires, a gruesome, lipless, mange-spotted lipodud on a sorrel-headed OHV spurts past.

Scene 2: A corpulent, flesh-rotten, completely hairless woman-height-figure, obscured by the cloud of dust, attracts the attention of the he-man, who unravels from a sand-dune with a sheaf of black parchment embroidered with his signature, above which the words MARRIAGE ANNULMENT are visibly printed.

Scene 3: The emaciated, stark-white body of a human mouse covered in scabs and splotches of gray hair. On the tip of the trident piercing its chest the black parchment like a flag flaps violently in the hissing desert wind. An owl with spongy human legs plods towards it.

Scene 4: A finely sculpted termite with skin the color of weak coffee and a blond pony head interprets from his single-cylinder ocarina the score of the words MARRIAGE ANNULMENT kabbalistically transliterated into music notes.

Scene 5: A yellow baby with a hulk's physique backhands a cream-corn-white crocodile with a copper mane, putting the croc in a headlock before suspending it from the edge of the Valles Marineris, the deepest canyon on Mars.

THE ADVENTURES OF MAN-WARRIOR

Scene 6: A fulsome, chalk-white *imitatrice* fissured with veins of verdigris, a thin beard of red fur extending to just below her belly, rides a haggard, almost hairless mare whose shoulders droop nastily, on the hunt for Reineke Fuchs, the human-fox with a velvet wit.

Scene 7: A husky, flat-faced, flabby-limbed farm girl, her armpits overflowing with stringy dishwater-colored hair like the crimped wires of tatty, grease-encrusted brillo pads, saunters across the desert on a grimy, balding, malnourished foal. Into the mouth of the torpedo-sized human-pig strolling on its leash beside her she spits a gob of tobacco juice from a rancid maw encrusted with dried lusterless red-black blood.

Scene 8: A sylph-like, well-preserved *grande dame* in the rococo theater halls of mid-life, crowned with a pyramid of diamonds. She twists her smooth, oriental whiskers atop a three-humped camel with a sleek tawny amber coat, spritzing with perfume the human-faced rabbits popping about its feet.

Scene 9: A nubile sun-bronzed waxen figure; a firm physique rising out of the oily magma the volcano neglected to properly mix. Impoverished puck-dancers ring the molten spire distilling their idol from its crater, banging on drums as they dance hysterically, summoning elephants who salivate from their gaping jaws as they blow human voices through their trunks painted with berries the color of a cloudless sunset.

Scene 10: A storky city girl, accustomed to all the accessories of compartmentalized city life, walks under a billboard with a man's gut on it, on his grease-stained tanktop the word MEDICINE is printed. He climbs down, literally a poster-child for male pattern baldness, his breath a septic miasma of undigested cream-cheese, vinegar and sausage, wilting the city girl's crystal mane until she is nothing but a human shadow chameleonically blending into the nightfall.

THE WOMEN OF MAN-WARRIOR

Scene 11: A dwarf the size of a full-grown man, his posture flaccid, disinterested, resembling in his carriage a deflated porpoise, looks into the emerald scope of his magic gun, perceiving through its lens two sets of Siamese twins riding sleek blue roans followed by a human-sized iguana fizzing brown cola from its jaws.

Scene 12: On a sand-colored stallion a slim hairless elf whistles a Jupiterian entoptic lullaby, pulling behind on a wooden cart enormous spools of freshly harvested wheat. The Elf's band, a human-lemur and a lynx-man from the afterlife, jangle their necklaces of teeth in time to the music, sipping unfinished gin and delta dust from silver thimbles.

Scene 13: A man who is a tattoo with stunning pectoral muscles and the arms and legs of a hero, yet with an over-engorged gut like a sphere of jelly suspended from a cliffside protruding out from under his tattoo of an undershirt with the words NOBODY WANTS THE UGLY WAITRESS printed on it, wrestles a mustang in a river of laxative and butterscotch, its currents soon consumed by doves until the river is nothing more than bleating beaks and flapping wings.

Scene 14: A handsome ugly man with a blotchy, monstrous Clydesdale head and mane like wires of dirty snow, his body sown from dung-colored jackal pelts, drives the rotten barrel of his tonka tank towards a set of identical twins, both female, one human, one lupine.

Scene 15: A sadistic male centaur, his taut baked-brown finely-etched construction hard pan of a figure testing out a thin, extraordinarily diminutive chicken-call; from the lustrous cream-orange sky above a startled leopard-woman astride Siamese twin Arabian stallions descends into the field of straw where the centaur is flailing.

THE SPECTACLE OF THE SIMULATION: THE ENEMIES OF MAN-WARRIOR

Scene 16: An ancient nag, nothing but wrinkled membrane with an oriental hue threatening to dissolve into dust at any moment, her head that of an out-sized brindle thoroughbred. She spins from her womb in a web of black rayon a row of polysynthetic twins: badger-human action figures.

Scene 17: A luminescent gamine spryly traipsing through an apple orchard in blossom, a sweet, if bulky, strawberry Shetland trailing the woman. The sun in its vertex delivers to her two hippopotamuses, binary duplicates conjoined in a locket of gold.

Scene 18: A post-belief body in a tear-stained lozenge of satin latex: a bituminous visage wound like the purple creases round the knuckles of a fighter's finger. On a strip of black parchment the face reads a comic about a set of identical twins, a trout male and a female human.

Scene 19: Infinity bobbing disproportionately on a minute toy horse, the lavender-scented plastic melting away into the delirious synthetic halos of a fiber-optic sunset. Stranded on a beach from which the epicenter of both duality and non-duality emanates, the epicene tears of twins without body neither lighten nor darken the screen.

Scene 20: The last female to give birth: a giant human slum containing several different ecosystems crowned with the head of a blueish-white American Arabian foal flops into a death-wreaking grotto by a stark abandoned roadway revealed at maximum resolution. From this emerges a series of repeated twins: hermaphroditic shape-shifters.

Io: After all I've done, this is how you repay me?

Adam: Forget them all.

Io: I see no other choice.

9

STRATAGEM DIANA

Neon streamers in a black auditorium. Ronald Reagan, *that beautiful man: a standard haircut.* George H.W. Bush, *organizer of the* CIA *coup that has just established him as* President of Human-Money Reality *and its* Star Wars *program: the same. They are searching for a hierarchical order through the moonlight.*

Bush: Even our thoughts are made in China ...

Reagan: If that's what it's going to take to break up the strike in Geneva, so be it.

Bush (*fingering a maquette of* New York City): The universalization of the false is the falsification of the universe. To put it in mortal terms: some nice looking things get the wrong idea from time to time. We need to open that large hadron portal to the underworld or wherever it goes before somebody else does.

Reagan: Certainly before they're wheeling me around like a machine of human entrails playing passive not to go berserk. I know they want to tell the world who I am when I'm not around, but even I don't know that. If one is to appear to return to the audience, one must first appear to grant the audience an audience.

Bush: They tell me they have no interest in you, though they assure me you are no common vector, no rebel suspended by principal, no feminine enemy of the hundred dollar bill, the dissipating center-web in a network of empty battery acid havoc. They say you are a criminal, that your crimes are sanctioned by the state, that Hell is the exact science contained in both our characters, and that you cannot be embarrassed. That is all.

Reagan: They say I have a grasshopper's body with a pickled diamond for a head. Anything further they will not designate.

Bush: Then I will interpret your grasshopper dream and the pickled substance of the gold standard, for every informant comes complete with vexation: if you inform on yourself to yourself, the costliest enterprises are accomplished in a single afternoon, yet you must punish yourself severely for torturing yourself. Through clandestine means we are planning to infiltrate a radical cell. Outside the forum we protest beside our adversaries while I deliver my address. If they prove too timid for violence, we take matters into our own hands. If this was indeed a condition of overbearance, we would instead alienate them one by one then recruit replacements from amongst the lowest caste.

Reagan (*writing a cheque for* 1¢.): Of course, that was all quite vivid, pure window dressing, *and God suffered the righteous to be slain*. There's no such thing as 'civilians'. From what I could tell, the computations of flamboyant, unmitigated chauvinism were civil.

Bush: It is no longer possible to believe anything one has not learned directly for themselves.

Reagan: Ribald. Ethereal.

Bush: The world can be a cruel place to be an honest man.

Reagan: No, and neither are you.

Bush: *Scelera non ulcisceris, nisi vincis:* You cannot say you have avenged a crime until you have bettered it. Did you hear that Gorbachev's birthmark is a blueprint of the Universe?

Reagan: The Whole Earth Catalog.

Bush: A modern utopia.

Reagan: Every organic utopia is a mechanical dystopia.

Bush: An autocrat entrenched in pure lucidity employed in matters touching the benefit of his country.

Reagan: Ariel Sharon says iniquity is the cause for the love of glory and the vain things of this world.

Bush: One must learn to betray even the art of betrayal, playing two roles simultaneously, then reversing them.

Reagan: I lock myself in a dungeon then command my immediate release . . .

Bush: With all that skill and practicability, you've acquired the precision of a surgeon general's warning.

Reagan: Or a secretary. They call me the *hearsay*-arch.

Bush (*perusing a copy of* Seneca's *The Spectacle of Society*): *A moderate man may win sincere approval; it takes a strong man to enforce feigned praise. Men must be made to want what they dislike* . . .

Reagan: *Qui notus nimis omnibus ignotus moritur sibi:* Death's terrors are for him who, too well known, will die a stranger to himself alone.

Bush: *The sword of Justice doth hang over you; yea, and it shall fall upon you and visit you to your utter destruction.*

Reagan: Let the wailing begin! Offstage, we follow a pitiful thaumaturge to his dressing room. Standing in his mirror we ask, *Do you think you can still operate Love?* After we take off our mask, he replies: *I can't help what I am, even if it is just a slogan.*

Bush: If she looks back she's interested.

Reagan: Is existence a metaphor for the universe? Is the human couple the supreme metaphor, the intersection of all forces, the seed of all forms?

Bush: Lead them to the future without them!

Reagan: He could, if he knew what he was. The only thing he is sure of is that he is aware of the exact opposite of everything.

Bush (*imagining himself as the lead in a movie in which the president is a* CIA *assassin leaving a trail of mechanical human wreckage in his wake and eventually landing a gig as his own body guard while hunting a low-level clerk whom he tells, 'I have the* Esquire *magazine article about you and all the other agents who were there that day. So sad how your wife left you and took your little daughter, and you were so forthright about your drinking. I was so moved by your honesty.'*): I ruined the secret service because I wanted to protect people. There's no cause worth fighting for: all we have left is the game.

Reagan: You are not a worshiper of God, but an operator who manages to impose his will on the material world.

Bush: Every culture and every civilization is but a Tower of Babel.

Reagan: The purpose of the play is to play itself; the meaning of the play is the play itself.

Bush: Family Generative Purpose.

Reagan (*watching himself in a cartoon variety show that never existed*): Let's not fall into the trap with him. We are free—free to fall into the same old trap of thinking we're free.

Bush: From the ceiling, arriving at a great distance, our eyes are here yet their sight is not merely where they are: it is, namely, *there*. It is all affectation, mannerism, inflection and inflation.

Reagan: Man, the great mimic and artificer of man.

Bush: That is what we will remember about each other and other men.

Bush: Enough to eat one?

Reagan: Do you have one to eat?

Bush: Just a little robot-legged fellow with a gun.

Reagan: He looks like an appetizer, not a meal.

Bush: He is Adam, the bounty-hunting scientist we blew up on the *Subject Predicate Object* in order to reassemble him as a cyborg super-soldier and use the footage of the explosion to promote the Star Wars think-tank incubator start up.

Reagan: A program that not only preempts inter-galactic war, but projects it.

Bush: We used Gorbachev's birthmark not only as a map of the fifth dimension, but as a schematic for the ship we blew up, the bomb we detonated to blow it up, and as a blue-print for the reconstruction of our cyborg scientist super-soldier, codename Adam Trillions, and as a template for the gene-editing armor with accellerant we outfitted him with pre-re-inception.

Reagan: We should eject him into space to find its core.

Bush: I believe it will be too loud.

Reagan: Then we should doom him to an iron dodecahedron-style prison temple where he can hear the children crying to be terminated.

Bush: Our horrors we must resume . . .

Reagan: Your physical disfigurement of having to wear eyeglasses proves that you are much more adept at this business than I. Let me tell you something in private: You make an obscenity of all you touch.

Bush: An ember burns in my breast for all I've exposed to the travesty of my mind, yet I feel no remorse.

Reagan: I agree. Let us treat our bionic compatriot with a glimpse into the abyss.

Bush: It will help us roast his cybernetic blood, as they say in Hollywood.

Reagan: Should we combine our minds to make barbecue sauce?

Bush: There is no other way.

An escape pod trailing party streamers ejects out across the stars. A single pink birthday candle is placed on a life-size model of the globe then lit. Adam is brought in on a stretcher, his head leaking a thin rope of brain tissue intertwined with crepe filling.

Reagan: Let us know how it tastes.

Bush, suddenly filled with upper-body strength, pries open Adam's mouth, spooning the brain tissue and crepe filling into it.

Adam: It tastes like an unlit fuse.

Reagan: The darkness gains, feeds. H.W. nods his face, his head remaining still. Adam exerts, stops. I ponder his welts, those rose-mouthed abrasions merging on his battered torso. In a most serious fashion I remove my eyes, polish them with Pepsi, re-insert them. I tell Adam it is time for the chase. He bellows: a swollen eructation that buds like a mushroom.

Bush: Doesn't this strike you as a bit too poignant of a moment to impose, let alone propose, release?

Adam: Hypocrites.

Reagan: Society gave us ethics, now we give them back.

Adam: Just like the cartography of Venus, I would have noticed if I were you.

Reagan: Are we too clever to trick you?

Adam: *Panem et circenses.* Humiliating, yet invigorating. Can you hear the world ... simmering?

Reagan: Sizzling like an aquifer, boiling away in the cosmic grammar of God's language.

Bush: *Such are the passions,* say the slaughters we celebrate.

Reagan: The celibate, sneering laughter.

Bush: Our shackles want to remain, to stand before the delusions of the galaxy crawling all over the their anorexic squeals. The hunt is a factory. Whether you run or not is irrelevant.

Reagan (*stuffing a hot dog into a potato as if it were a bun*): We wish to be judged by our enemies, if only superficially, yet we are not curious to hear what they have to say, for we are told it is inauspicious to prognosticate, and so we provide ourselves with their first opinions.

Bush: And in their opinion they have no opinion.

Reagan: That is the only cure for sunburn, or lynching.

Bush: He obviously does not want to be loosed upon Alpha Centauri. I suggest we cook him where he lies, as we do all our operatives.

Reagan: This has been a lecture on *Gastronomie de luxe.*

Bush: You're not as stupid as you were before you said that. I would rather serve my country on a platter a hundred times over than fight for what's right just once. They say

STRATAGEM DIANA

I am a charitable man when it comes to stealing. I have vast storehouses full of treasure I've squandered. Adam, Ronald, I would rather climb a conifer than confer with such irritating momentary template-humans. If you can withstand seeing what everyone but yourself can see, again, then unlock this child-like man-god and his mesocratic effluvia! His pus alone reveals a diversity of life unparalleled elsewhere, though not as popular as what can be found in, say, Tartarus, Tartary, Metatron's Navel or the Marianas Trench, or any other transcendental slob-soul tourist attraction, which can teach us all it wants, if it wants.

Adam: Grant me my freedom.

Reagan: The truth is, there's no such thing as "bad guys".

Bush: Your biological extremity transfixes the ghost inside me.

Adam *is uncuffed.*

Adam: I'm clean. I can pump my fist and believe in the labor party.

Bush: Or simply exterminate them with or without going into battle.

Adam: Wouldn't you prefer to see me slick my hair back instead?

Bush: Only if it establishes a correlation between a lack of hygiene in the barracks and encephalitis.

Adam: *Carte blanche vox populi.* Is that correlation enough?

Reagan: If I witness it with my own eyes. H.W., replace your friend here in the shackles. Recite your spinal fluid.

Bush: Certainly. Would you have me face the flag?

Reagan: Is that not self-evident?

Adam: He's just upset he can't perform murder.

Bush: Whispered impressions.

Reagan: I no longer feel the desire to impress upon anyone the things I believe—maybe because I no longer believe them—maybe because I no longer believe anything. Maybe I am afraid of what I believe—no more simple an answer could exist. The urge may have overwhelmed me and now all I do is indoctrinate others with what I no longer believe. To achieve the terminus yet still continue: the future is there, too clever for itself, thus you must ignore it if it is to be revealed. I, on the other hand, no longer wish to be clever. Once you have been the labyrinth you will never exit yourself. Who can wish that they were blind? It all started from memory, both decay and growth; Dante could not have found Beatrice in hell—*or perhaps that is the only place he could have found her?*—for she was his heaven. Answering the question of who we are answers all other questions.

Is it dust flavored? Is it America flavored? Mutilated in the war like a country ditty, only our shadows breathe in the dead city laid out before us. *Across the expanse of God's great creation/Dentures chew the last particle of a geriatric gas station. What is all this horror behind the forest green?*, your girlfriend asked the president of the Motion Picture Association of America, the highest office on Earth. If I get *more*, is that the *more* I *want?* A little bit of unconscious sunlight should do the trick. The Earth is a sphere: there's no direction. Only my vote counts: there's no election.

Shazam shim kaput. You can only see black magic in the lantern and the soot. Maybe your shadow is not telling you the truth. *Why would a shadow lie?* Because it loves you. Through the medicine cabinet of well-organized pareidolia, I never had the chance to be anything but a spy kit in the hands of the divine. Using the human frequency control signal, we arranged JFK's deathwish, assassination, and resurrection. Saudi Aramco? Silent Running? They can kill my voice, but there's a million more exactly like it. Remember Adam, through the metal glimmering like stars the bent debris of his body being recomposed? Someday this veneer of mystification will pay off with the words the Earth created. *After all this endless prevaricating, who would dare suggest there was something worth elucidating?* He's a Hiroshima bore seeking the simulation of a reprocessed court reporter.

Bush: A stunning likeness.

Adam: You can keep talking, just keep your thoughts to yourself.

Reagan: You're either a weapon of the opposition, or the opposite of a weapon.

Adam: Many believe you are either overburdened with gaiety or just opposed to the marriage of a cyborg to a coffee pot. The Prime Thesis was not authored by an impostor. Last year you claimed to have a seductive glint in your eye which proved you could engage in hand to hand combat while still retaining your ethical values. I have that moment memorized. Would you like it reproduced?

Reagan: After the world dies.

Bush: That is an insinuation in progress.

Adam: I recognized him by the smell of his titular weapon, the Raygun. When I entered his tent he was flustered, studying an ancient Japanese wood etching of a peacock lain under a guillotine somewhere in Egypt. He looked into my eyes then looked away, searching for the severed head. Apparently the avian princess had survived, an agreement we tacitly formed when he ran me through with the hilt of his broadsword. His place wasn't very clean, neither was the desert in which it sat. I bumped against an arid hill of plastic and he accused me of being too rigid. I called him a stiff and accused him of behaving dissolutely towards a picture of a blue sodium chloride crystal I'd brought him from "that Asiatic city of innumerable churches, holy Moscow." He made me lick the picture to demonstrate how tasteless it was, then tossed it into a chest full of Russian nesting owls, a third in scale, or so he claimed. I accelerated my whole mass and damaged his ego. He tried to stand, but his skin had turned to vapor and there were green gases seeping out of his chest. One of the owls launched out of its nest like a missile, blowing me to pieces. I noticed that the plumage of the peacock on the etching had received a delicate roseate hue from my blood, so I declared the interlude acclaimed.

Reagan: *Vox populi, vox dei.* A fascinating iteration. You may call me Uncle, or the man therefrom, at least in front of him. I can hear a wren with an ophidian voice say, *This is becoming.*

10

ARTIFICE APOLLO

Loxias: Some intemporal things might get the wrong impression from time to time. I know it as I know myself I do.

Phoebus: We neutrally contrast, I a bit sharper than you.

Loxias: I: sharper and duller than both.

Phoebus: Irrefutable, yet one would hesitate to call it certain.

Loxias: We turn, then we redouble.

Phoebus: Vinous resplendence, radiance, vision, double-vision; misery recast as exaltation: through the lens they cling to a vacant sphere of sun.

Loxias: Sustained in condemnation . . .

Phoebus: Manifold and August . . .

Loxias: It augments with silence . . .

Phoebus: The radiation of one to the next . . .

Loxias: *Cut is the branch that might have grown full straight and burned in Apollo's laurel bough . . .*

Phoebus: *Too long, too well I know the starry conclave of the midnight sun, too well the splendors of the firmament . . .*

Loxias: Too needful to look upon to look upon. The rendition . . .

Phoebus: . . . in silence . . .

Loxias: . . . vituperating . . . venality in justice . . .

Phoebus: The causality turns in the eyes of the other . . .

Loxias: A mutant sunflower is dissolved to impart . . .

Phoebus: . . . the iliac crest of a youthful reflection . . .

Loxias: . . . alone . . .

Phoebus: . . . with everything.

Loxias: *Terminat hora diem; terminant autor opus.*

Phoebus: . . . and lingers in a song . . .

(*tuning their lyres:*)

Loxias: It happens they share a cadence . . .

Phoebus: Who would happen to have been born the others . . .

Loxias: A mute ancestry . . .

Phoebus: *How can the ghostly guidance fail? Whereby my prophet's soul is lead, look-for their eyes the spector children wail, their sodden nerves on which their father's fed.*

ARTIFICE APOLLO

Loxias: *Apollo, Apollo, God of all ways, but death alone to me.*

Phoebus: Make them abstemious ...

Loxias: Remove their dazzle of self-shrine and anointment ...

Phoebus: *He well might boast him now a second Geryon, of triple frame with triple robe of earth above him laid, for that below, no matter how triple dead, dead by one death for every form he bore.*

Loxias: The body of refuge a refugee in the body ...

Phoebus: What will they play upon their lyre?

Loxias: Ormolu.

Phoebus: Let us oblige them ...

Loxias: The sun looks upon itself in the eye of another sun from the haze of the water below ...

Phoebus: The sun casts no shadow yet itself as a clock ...

Loxias: Obviating the repetitious, stating without record, assignations here and here, the light of our blood ...

Phoebus: ... before it is time to close the sun ...

Loxias: A rush of gold over the wind where the cithara chime and stall ...

Phoebus: ... the Before-Time is stayed ...

Loxias: Who is absence and who is arrival and where in the sand do they vanish?

Phoebus: The wind-polished root of a lattice of helix . . .

Loxias: . . . in bone as in sand, the string's eternal provision . . .

Phoebus: . . . forever paired, their embrace, a void the hours insert and encircle, asking who will await . . .

Loxias: An acquittal . . .

Phoebus: . . . the rays in Tartarus . . .

Loxias: . . . proscribed . . .

Phoebus: . . . their claws in gold damask . . .

Loxias: . . . the gold separates . . .

Phoebus: Prove this—

Loxias: They listen with excitement; they weigh the pause unborn . . .

Phoebus: . . . they weigh the pause stillborn . . .

Loxias: We are not listening. The voice separates.

Phoebus: Nothing is known, there is nothing to prove, nothing is grown. To them, how can we prove this?

Loxias: Prove the muscles of a swan . . .

Phoebus: The enchanter's arms out-crossed . . .

Loxias: The slogan of the refinished dawn . . .

Phoebus: . . . rising on the periphery. We stay where we are most beseeched, braiding the pace of our tones, staging the ligaments of commerce we are beseeched to stage; braided, now vanished in the future of the haze . . .

Loxias: . . . in vestures of the near-future: the structure of the eagle's ashes twining through the lichen at dusk . . .

Phoebus: . . . recalled to anyone who beckons . . .

Loxias: . . . temporary and bouyant as the gold green . . .

Phoebus: . . . of deteriorated Time and the sacramental impurities of the world . . .

Loxias: . . . vanished in the crowd, a half-vision . . .

Phoebus: . . . everlasting mirage . . .

Loxias: . . . and illustrious soul unconquered . . .

Phoebus: . . . unused . . .

Loxias: . . . projected through the elements . . .

Phoebus: . . . demeaned by the idle . . .

Loxias: . . . praised by the demeaned . . .

Phoebus: . . . compiled with . . .

Loxias: . . . asked and unanswered . . .

Phoebus: . . . and the living will have their equalities of death . . .

Loxias: . . . their memories the least commitment . . .

Phoebus: . . . beyond unmentionable variances . . .

Loxias: . . . till the erasure of variance . . .

Phoebus: . . . obsessing their outmoded para . . . ?

Loxias: —dice.

Phoebus: Outscrolling from the hand of God . . .

Loxias: . . . the eternal denial . . .

Phoebus: . . . of substance . . .

Loxias: . . . thus he gives . . .

Phoebus: . . . his consent . . .

Loxias: . . . and Will subordinates . . .

Phoebus: . . . to Truth . . .

Loxias: . . . in the microspan of a zeptosecond!

Phoebus: . . . an alluvial deposit . . .

Loxias: . . . bifurcates . . .

Phoebus: . . . devoid of ornament . . .

Loxias: . . . flavescent . . .

Phoebus: . . . uterine . . .

Loxias: . . . pouring down like skin . . .

Phoebus: . . . apically symmetric . . .

Loxias: . . . a diamond of charity . . .

Phoebus: . . . ornamentation . . .

Loxias: . . . the sun pours down . . .

Phoebus: . . . all is equal . . .

Loxias: . . . a statistical present . . .

Phoebus: . . . the voice of ineradicable order . . .

Loxias: . . . the light stored in a billion . . .

Phoebus: . . . crystalline tombs of stars . . .

Loxias: . . . bereavement and reproduction . . .

Phoebus: . . . pity . . .

Loxias: . . . and unequivocal pain . . .

Phoebus: . . . the sun pours down . . .

Loxias: . . . someone must have finished . . .

Phoebus: . . . before they were . . .

Loxias: . . . like skin . . .

Phoebus: . . . freshly adopted . . .

Loxias: . . . formlessly giving orders . . .

Phoebus: . . . at the edge of perceptible time . . .

Loxias: . . . a pulsar uncoupled from Time . . .

Phoebus: . . . and those we resume, bereaved of imagined light . . .

Loxias: . . . the circle ensconced . . .

Phoebus: . . . and solar reprieve . . .

Loxias: ... polished and uni-variant ...

Phoebus: It is pity granted their image in the glass ...

Loxias: ... the bio-sidereal retreat ...

Phoebus: ... of electricity into invention ...

Loxias: ... thus they shall, till the olden new ...

Phoebus: ... shall they not?

Loxias: Reconfigured within the prisons of a barren wish ...

Phoebus: They bargain with the authority to have done with doing ...

Loxias: ... and those who would like it known they are under no obligation to be ...

Phoebus: ... they elevate the dyskinesia's specter ...

Loxias: ... to a specter of autonomy ...

Phoebus: ... to supplement their offerings with service ...

Loxias: ... to serve their offerings ...

Phoebus: ... with honor and impotence ...

Loxias: ... the actor an inevitable celestial derivative ...

Phoebus: ... two coins the same side divined ...

Loxias: ... cerebral, spurious, conjoined ...

Phoebus: ... the sun in the hair and yellow wine ...

Loxias: . . . the aromatic fumes of every perspective . . .

Phoebus: . . . the preeminent taste . . .

Loxias: . . . the white vulture overspreads the world . . .

Phoebus: . . . Grecian luxury, haughtiness, abomination . . .

Loxias: . . . garlands of Roman emptiness bedeck the vacant embassies where Reality detached their minds . . .

Phoebus: . . . the thief detached a star from his diamond's face . . .

Loxias: . . . and ascertained what nothing can exhibit . . .

Phoebus: . . . not enough can be uttered yet nothing can be said . . .

Loxias: . . . the synodic period of omnibodiment . . .

Phoebus: . . . the perihelion's task complete . . .

Loxias: . . . atrocity . . .

Phoebus: . . . purity's first form . . .

Loxias: . . . the piety of first generation . . .

Phoebus: . . . luxuriating in origin . . .

Loxias: . . . purity's duplicate . . .

Phoebus: . . . complete . . .

Loxias: . . . they stand trial unaccused . . .

Phoebus: . . . the customary declamations . . .

Loxias: . . . the smell of sunlight . . .

Phoebus: . . . must be accomplished before it's designed . . .

Loxias: . . . before the law is outside itself . . .

Phoebus: . . . the erasure must be unlocked before it is hidden . . .

Loxias: . . . severance must be enjoyed before it is granted . . .

Phoebus: . . . ointment must be sharpened before it soothes . . .

Loxias: . . . before the ray came the nexus . . .

Phoebus: . . . all maxims of coinage . . .

Loxias: . . . the camera focuses the eye . . .

Phoebus: . . . containing every eye it has gazed into . . .

Loxias: . . . the sun on every face . . .

Phoebus: . . . the melody of such axioms . . .

Loxias: . . . spinning in their native spheres . . .

Phoebus: . . . in stunning flash and agility . . .

Loxias: . . . the fertile bow overdraws the lyre . . .

Phoebus: . . . the chevron assimilates all representation of fragrance . . .

Loxias: . . . photons rained and washed the air . . .

Phoebus: . . . Praedicamenta . . .

Loxias: . . . a semantic pre-bodiment of substance, quantity, relation, place, time, position, state, action, affection . . .

Phoebus: . . . the flare indrawn externally ordered . . .

Loxias: . . . to bind the ether . . .

Phoebus: . . . on our way . . .

Loxias: . . . the departure . . .

Phoebus: . . . we bred in our wings . . .

Loxias: . . . the waste of too much arrival . . .

Phoebus: . . . too grand the course of a shattered string . . .

Loxias: . . . the all-wanted, the barren fruit's new nectar . . .

Phoebus: . . . to bare the seed, the thinning apex of such a vivid dream . . .

Loxias: . . . the face rotates . . .

Phoebus: . . . distinct the mirror from no reflection . . .

Loxias: . . . the tower of autumn hesitates . . .

Phoebus: . . . the fresh mystery . . .

Loxias: . . . motionless in the distant gold . . .

Phoebus: . . . revolving . . .

Loxias: . . . the burning drama . . .

Phoebus: . . . fused to the season's glory . . .

Loxias: ...preview...

Phoebus: ... the spectacle integrates...

Loxias: ... preserved and invented...

Phoebus: ... reified the tearless band...

Loxias: ... the aperture recollects, edits, binds it...

Phoebus: ... the light sheds it's sympathy...

Loxias: ... rarefied, the toneless banned...

Phoebus: ... gleaming conductions...

Loxias: ... sound abdicates...

Phoebus: ... the odor of fusion...

Loxias: ... fission's attar...

Phoebus: ... the luminous betrothed...

Loxias: ... the burial betrothed...

Phoebus: ... cinders of the tongue...

Loxias: ... mute and incandescent...

Phoebus: ... champion...

Loxias: ... white gold the trophy...

Phoebus: ... the trophy of thy teeth...

Loxias: ... where the light becomes purer...

Phoebus: ... scission with all...

ARTIFICE APOLLO

Loxias: . . . murmurous, everlasting . . .

Phoebus: . . . a state unoccupied . . .

Loxias: Which aspect prevails?

Phoebus: The automated universe . . .

Loxias: The universal truth of automated belief?

Phoebus: The absence introduced . . .

Loxias: . . . absolute and somewhat . . .

Phoebus: . . . counter-circuitous . . .

Loxias: They change the skin on the light . . .

Phoebus: . . . their garments elemental clairaudience . . .

Loxias: . . . half-synthesis, half-silence . . .

Phoebus: . . . the solution to a voice's half-timbre . . .

Loxias: . . . dual synthetic radiance unchoosing . . .

Phoebus: The sun looks up from the water to find another sun . . .

Loxias: Half-monochrome, half-rapture; half discourse on the whole; half-greeting, half-report, half apology; half-farewell, half-attack; half-human, half demi-god . . .

Phoebus: The end—

Loxias: The dialogue of the two systems—

Phoebus: . . . the eternal return . . .

11

THE JUNO HERESY

Address the remainderrrrrrrrrrrrrrrrrrrrrrrrrrrrrrrrrrrrrrroooooooooooo ooooooooooooooooooof the person. TTTTTTTTTTTTTTTTThe appetitive vigil. The pneumatic midnighttttttttttttttttttttttttttttttttttttttttttttttttttt. RRRRRRRRRReified augury in support of what you must . . . what you must never knowwww. WWW WWWhat you believe is positive and negative stasissssssssssssssssssssssssssssssssssssssssssssssssssssssssss. NNNNNNNNNNNNNNNNNNNNNNNNNNNNNNNN NNNNNNNNNNNNNNNNNNNNNNNNNever interrupt. NNNNNNeeeeeeverr aask whoose woorrks theese miiight haaave beeeeeeeeeeeeennnnnnnnnnnnnnnnn.

The inborn universality clings.

The mural that escaped stares across composite: voice spliced to counter-node. Mortal strictures. The mark of the bought.

The sign of the sold. The violator's exhibition.

In the clamped jaws of the Colonia Bizarre.

The station, suspended from the early morning.

Military viscera.

Smoke. Foreign soil.

Dead Eclipse. The exclusive

dodecadent.

The principate, the glass ceiling,

the glass nest:

VOID IN ALL STATES.

Rotate.

Am I?

Approaching? No.

I AM.

Take what might have been for what never . . .

Secede.

<How it stuns.>

<Look at him.>

<One with and one

withheld.>

<Let him.>

<Him?>

<Materialize.>

<His body.>

<His armor.>

<Warped.>

<It? That?>

A shoulderless leaning into the facet.

Against this we are this.

The beach.

The cheroot in his face. *It's Time I like.*

\

The ghost I ask, *When is truth?*

Our vision or their non-re-vision?

Theft of immersive prestige.

A capacity for subcritical design—

Data quantitation.

Are we ashamed to be seen or unseen?

Man: The Perfected Optic.

Cyberoptic pathogens.

On every leaf.

Posing.

Would you like to undream that?

<*How?*>

Spring's fundamental diaspora. Elution.

Chromatography.

Stoichiometry.

Intrigue.

Laments of the demimonde.

Liaison. Omen.

Chameleonic poisons, poison chameleons.

TTTTTThe cremation of Neeeeeeeeeeeeeeeeeeeeeeeeeeeeeeeeeeeeeeeeeeeeeeeeeee eeeeeeeeeeeeeed. AAAAAAAAAAAAAAAAAAll of this and mooooooooooooooooooorrrrrrrrrrrrrrrrrrrrrrrrrrrrrrrrrrrrrr e. TTTThe Play Space of Idiotsssssssssssssssssssssssssssssssssssssssssssssssssssssssssss sssssssssssssssssssssss. AAAAAAAAAAAAAAAAAAAAAAAAAAAAAAAAAAAAAAAA

AAAAAAAAAAAAAApppear to Be. *A smooth-angled process where things first find that delete.*

People fanatic voids.

Perpetual neutrals. Choice or choosing.

What it is happens.

Bred to circuits.

. . . I ask myself.

One minute in the fragments of a public service announcement.

Exposure. Seeing in as out.

An entire culture at a back-glance.

. . . in a few ungiven syllables.

With regard to journalists . . .

This is why we don't give what-not to whom.

If we remain objective, ethics are money.

. . . devoid of unbidden opinion.

Thus I have, so I am.

So give us a few what-have-you-nots.

. . . on Earth as we must our children . . .

. . . with others as ourselves . . .

We see we are at a stalemate without noticing it.

The land strives to respond.

                              Inferior is enough.

Presentiment is futile.

                              Issues of the F-Layer.

*To do so without it would allow silence to interrupt
silence.*

I ask only to live in harmony without myself or others.

. . .

ttttttttttttttttttttttttttttttttttttttttttttttttttttttttttttttttttttttttttttttt
ttttttttttttttttttttttttttttttttttttttttto ooo *make the stage
hiiiivvvvve.*

The Adam must now sentence a judge who has been
accused of deviating from Time. There is little doubt as to
the defendant's guilt. The society the Adam represents
refuses to ascertain the circumstances that led the judge to
perpetrating such an ignominious crime. Society desires
the judge abolished. The Adam carries out their orders. A
citizen sees this and they say nothing, fearing they will
only be giving voice to moot opinions, that their peers will
shun them, despise them, that in speaking out they will be
seen as someone who believes they are above the fear they
stir. The people fear the Adam as they fear their inde-
pendence. They have neutralized themselves, and the
citizen who would speak becomes the scapegoat for all
their repressed impulses, the victim of all their aborted
transformations. They know the Adam is too powerful
from the way everyone, including themselves, zealously
authenticates its power. The citizen is common, like the
others, and a much easier target: no one sanctions their

authority as an individual: they are no leader. Who is the citizen to presume to function as such? They are nominal, disposable. Knowing this, they remain silent. In doing so they gain the pretended respect of the other citizens, until one day it is their child who becomes an Adam and must accuse the judge. Then the citizen speaks out. It is not the judge's fault, nor the Adam's, nor the child's. The child's first order as Adam is to execute all children. No one says a thing.

IT IS ALWAYS LANGUAGE SPEAKING THROUGH A NETWORK OF INFINITE ANONYMOUS CITATIONS

What mute deity re-enters with such treachery, suspended by these obscene wonders? What betrayed birth has less than sin? In this age, Man clamors in his own image to become God's savior. It is time for the body of Christ to reject this idolatry of men masquerading as saviors. They are conscious of not having passed on to their descendants, nor of having fulfilled the decrees of God, saying, All . . .

I cannot imagine this going to plan. Floating cliffs, an acclivity like the smile of an unconquerable mountaineer, the face over the face. He takes a bottle of green water and pours some into the plastic cup of his hand. *What am I doing?* he believes he wonders. Motion redressed. There is no pulse. There is no charge, positive. Fatigue maneuvers fatigue. I need a more systematic approach, a stunning military fantasy, a silent almanac that awaits wherever I go. I make a systematic and rational approach to the next thing, wherever you are, and I am pleasantly surprised by my openness to the way forward. What I have to do is live: it's that simple. I sit next to a mystic on a bus and look at my computer screen: Gone. Impressive water.

−You told me who told you who told me you met a man, a proletariat bald guru with the word NO tattooed on a representation of his ankle in a tiny scroll that may or may not exist but could be shown by his successor. −I may have, but only because I lack the proper social mechanisms to make an excuse for the scene from the orbiter. −Never. −From then until our dust. −The situational acromegalics spindle, your Imminence. They lack the legged fortitude of one told of this station. They bandy till the military re-enters and some guru endures it. −As do we. −If I have I have. −You and that potsmith fanaticism. −You interrupt me. −I am simply absorbing the background radiation and licking the sparks from an incinerating hologram, one whose toxic freedom creates an animosity between the object deprived of its reality and the subject who robbed it. −Your gunmetal teeth are attending a party in front of everyone gone dormant. −Metaphysically? −Meekly, majestically snarling orders at a trap, the chair pointing to the trap. −The obfuscation conjoins.

A courtroom. Consider a buffoon to be there. An insult, an insinuation, an institution, all as systematic as one's excrement, emblematizing a status one attains without one's knowledge. The switch drops. For no reason he can't be sentenced. His crimes will resurrect him. He has done what with whom or we have done what with whomsoever. How can this be? Just an off-handed figure punished with figurative handicraft. He just figured we'd kill each other. The summer a tunnel of electric flames in his mouth. Two birds cross: the butcher and the lamb leading itself to the slaughter.

There will be no more innocent behavior; there will be no more shock-and-awe purity. What's wrong with our intent? Why did we render so many models of a prison? Concrete stock-footage of the best teachers will not make it easier. Is it in the interest of those who sell novelty at any price to eradicate the means of measuring it? Dissemination, production, generation, acquisition: at their infinitesimal cores, what do these words mean?

. . . being who I am, I would first have to build a laugh before at last delivering it. Besides, it would render me bilious. Even then, I would still be proud to call you my brother. We must all compromise, even in the insect prison, where I earned my coveted limp. But now look at me, all fame and glory and self-annihilation, hanging my head like a corroded bronze of myself, a statue eaten by the years and its underwater prison scars. I still have fine nostrils, and my back is covered in coarse black tarturian plankton and gills like the tiles of the baths in an underground city abandoned long ago on White Mars. Perhaps this is why, when at the beach or the office, or wherever I bathe, it is all I can do to keep from being sterilized.

—*The mind/soul are the last thing we lose before becoming nothing.*—

—There was always the possibility you'd never be correct. If you were our brother Neptune, perhaps shrieking, we might find the brief remedy of release.—

—*Now you console me for my insult?*—

—You've forgotten the lesson: an insult is an accolade yet inverted. There's nothing else worth correlating to compromise.—

—*Is it ideal to possess a cloud of radon gas that transforms into the likeness of whomever it kills and have mankind march in and out of it, returning in the freshly polished bodies of their stripped, stark naked souls?—*

—Let us strive to hope . . . —

—Each day we grant ourselves the courage to wake up and face the morning.—

—I don't know what more could be asked.—

—Let us be cruel.—

—We have no choice; it is the estate we were born to. Should we trade it for the hovel or the pit?—

—Guilt is, after all, the most amorous nuisance our imaginations have seen fit to provide us. The remorseless beasts of the earth derive no exaltation from the crazed possession sequestered in its shadows.—

—That is why I want war with *Mars Original*, that sacrosanct flower of a human body burnt to ashes by its own blood, the dried cheeks of a head culminating in fructified dust.—

—Sacred astral metals calumniating, galloping over the scarred flesh, a refracted crystal of sunlight perched on the skeleton's visor, a symphony of carrion above a symphony of debris.—

—We will die to protect this desert.—

—Every image a calculated distortion, the harmony of the chaos like a burning swan evaporating in the dusk, the incorporeal horizon transparent layers of ever-shifting picture plane.—

—It is easy and pointless to recollect that night, the never-before-mixed particles effervescing in some water of S/space, Tartarus sauce applied, in honor of the conquest of Mayhem, or Maya, whatever and whenever the last deity we heard celebrated an event as a world holiday for latrines scrubbed to a glint, and the Mars of a Thousand Planets displayed in the affectation we must adopt to discuss it.—

—*Last night has been said on a frozen plane and the use of type-isolated deputations and axonometric projections has fructified the drought. A higher compliment could not be paid.*—

—The Miracle of the Mayflower, its preferred designation.—

—*That's the term Mesopotamian dentists applied to their long-sought-after toothpastecicles.*—

—Going in or coming out?—

—*I've lost track, the dream has gone on too long unfulfilled to be nullified. I've forgotten all but my shame.*—

—I've forgotten how to believe you.—

—*That is why you are nothing but a source of shame. Son of Mars, midwife to Jupiter, husband to all inactive accounts on Earth, your presence is an infirmity, a phantom limb of the celestial family.*—

—Except yourself.—

—*If you could somehow absent your personality from your neo-thoughts without further debt to the People of Forever, as well as their counterparts, the Personas of Never, I would not otherwise conform to myself.—*

—Tuck your soul into a blade of glass until your voice decides it is not false, preening, and what it will become. It is autumn after this, and the grass will soon be dead.—

—Not dead dear brother, mercifully dormant.—

Thus spake Ahriman and Ormuzd atop a dwindling candle's flame.

12

THE JANUS DRIVE

Bacteriological lights at all angles. Janus, the god of duplicity, has generated a third god through the synergistic interaction of his twin facades. The inoperative gaze, on the verge, the limit, nearing the farring, the boarder, the crossing bound, breached, stayed, bypassed, invoked, unassimilated, revoked, a wincing pause accumulated to lustration, beatific isonomy, a genteel and pathological portrait of Space, stifled, eclipsed, inward into oblate veins; inward, the outer tissue honed to a cast.

Janus: We will be as we will be.

The species has been sold.

Janus: There is no evidence. You wait for Time but it comes without you, and there you watch it waste through the scope of yourself as if it were yourself, as it is. You are the charade and the impostor perpetrating it. The correct amount of material. Looking back on you looking forward. Demonstrate anatomical heterodoxy only to the key which unlocks itself. I would speak, but I vacillate. There are so few flesh and blood people left in the world. Somewhere there is a void, fearful or fallow, unexhibited. That is, your honor, all that is extant, permitting the authorization of your martial quotient, the percentage graphic, the equivocant, the continuum from Justice to something

Nature finds more suitable: black electricity. Social acting, vertical disengagement, savagery, subliminal mortality, harried ascensions: these are the guarantees we provide the free market. The oligarchs, their lunar thrones, remain exempt from prosecution until they are dissolved.

Syncorp's progenitor is fond of harps and piercing. He has a list of chemical hastates he fills with wounds, with completely ignored filth: the poor. It takes unprecedented courage to dare the white spires of academic health: it takes anemia.

Janus: It is time for us to die. This is not my country, nor do I belong to it. Events transpire as they conspire to. We belong only to those who are willing to die for anything, dissipation foremost.

Circumnavigation. A vulture camera. A pentagonal hexecontahedron camera the size of Mars.

Janus: The drama plays out on its faces. It is our cowardice that makes it all seem so heroic. They, as we, are fused and separated by their fusion. Our emotions condemn themselves to be merely that: emotions. The future shall elevate these images to photographs.

[*Tar pits erupting out of the soul of the Earth; the souls of decent folk trying to flit by before they happen.*]

Janus: In the photograph you perceive three things: the photograph, the eye that took it, and yourself ascertaining. Through circumperception, you come closer to the image, until you see not only its master, but the camera that properly descried it, a rhombic dodecahedron planetoid hidden behind the moon, asphyxiating on a holo-gem artery, the infinite *in* and *of,* between its Self and itself. It is in love with both, as are we. The front page headline reads THERE GOES YOUR FRONT PAGE INTERVIEW next to a picture of silicate reaching for a seared respirator to find its face inside—only the face—burnt to a vapor-thin crust across the interior of the sealant rings and the visor, palpable only as ash to the touch. The doors of perception have been cleansed. Now we see the face of every man as it truly is: reversed, extinguished, barren, a place where nothing can be and anything can be nothing.

I've seen men die for their countries. Men who die for their children, for love: they die for nothing. Their greatest accomplishment is a digital photograph of themselves off weeping or screaming into eternity after an exquisite replay of the first film man ever saw. You will remember every court you fled from, every law you broke: lines, lice, and lies; your arts and sciences and wealth the master's lamentations reduced to a few starved eyes in the monitor. There is limitless reason to cry, waiting for decryption, effaced by what has been pawned-off as sentiment. Remember the words said in the beginning, in the golden inappetence before it was all confused: was this a flexible language or one carved in bone? A scripture of virtual vegetation? A transliteration of star's milk?

A battle ensues: the calamitous cartoon stripped to its reactor in an orchestra of cruciform illiteracy, tangent fields, windows bisecting, the net evaluation of coiled paraffin shredded across a degenerating plane, the frantic lights pregnant with this confetti of symbols that falls in every language. The blood flares and money the size of human fingernails acrobatically spirals through the alternating gels of the stage lights as the light grows more and more caustic through this analogue of vision, leaking jewel-colored oils in a roped relay with the music, the entire cast of every homecoming dance distilled into a single verse, an automatic vacancy that parts from its cosmetically mated cessation, the gels pouring in flesh-melting liquids of indigo, rose and honey, fried wires splaying from torched light sockets in this inauthentic replacement gravity. Faces materializing from figments of laughter. There is always someone behind you in the mirror, attending to the details, to be delivered.

IRONY AS A MEANS OF DEPRIVING THE OBJECT OF ITS REALITY IN ORDER THAT THE SUBJECT MAY FEEL FREE

Gen. Hating: The way to own someone is to not look at them, to keep them incomplete.

Dr. Tiresias: The most direct path to freedom is through remaining unseen.

At first it seems as if a stone will erode until we realize the weather is imitating it. The smooth blank stalactite: a statue with duplicating faces, one on back of the other, interlaid, overlaid, growing cold: fissure, chip, bake, crumble, rescind, respawn at origin, wash out and gray. A pocket with minuscule pools and quarries: here the lone hermaphrodites focus in incorporeal rings, dividing their progeny from themselves—who is who?—pursuing their thirsts under their imperceptible persuasions. The statue looks for itself. No harvest watch-keeper can see every element of the harrow. The people stop looking at the statue. They feel as if it has seen too much, as if one day it will open its mouth before the one who comes before death, the face extending in a tiled tapestry from their optic nerves to the constellations, the god who dresses them dwindling in each until they believe it is they who are diminished, the god—themselves—the infiltrator.

The idol has become indestructible. Then comes the visage famine: its traces germinate, grafted onto the shadow's ligaments, the undetectable schism between the many personalities of the pulse.

Janus: The people are surprised when one day the statue begins to shrink. It happens during fashion week. A renowned impresario by the name of Mania remarks that he has seen what appeared to be a diamond encrusted tar seeping from the idol's eyes. With a drill—unaccustomed in the absolute to the people's fear of what they've statured as an article of pure cosmic time-energy—he bores into the right eye of the face directed away from the city. The issue is collected in urns and rubbed on the legs of cripples, on the eyes of those who can't see, without their consent, and with the admonishment, *Go thou within thyself to ask the strangers of their tale,* infuriating the uncooperative recipients of this divine unction until they become belligerent, storming the maternity ward, cutting the throats of the babies and drinking their blood. Those who overdose are rushed to the inertiatic chamber, where an emulsion of mercury and belladonna is administered in a krypton bath. Benign pharmacology, sensory therapy, energy sculpting, telecolor: Mania's extravagant mannerisms and pretended courage gain him the position of Archimandrite over the garment district, a cluster of dilapidated shacks and sweatshops. He publicly cultivates an addiction to the diamond tar, bottling it to be sold for his consumption alone. He is regarded by the *couché couture* as indispensable. When rumors of a near death experience surge, the streets fill with remonstrating mannequins and their inconsolable heiresses slaughtering their prize studs and most expensive gowns to be seen expressing their agony. Dogs stop wearing jeweled collars.

Synthetics and hybrids abound. Marketed as Nxz, these facsimiles are nothing more than a few cubic zirconium a dead squid spat out. The genuine article is locked away, the statue, christened by its warders Astro Incitatus, the personification of a '66 Camaro, now nothing more than a hollowed-out blood-black talisman fitting into the palm of a dwarf's hand.

HE SAID HE WAS A COSMETIC PSYCHOLOGIST

A strange incident one night involving the talisman: Though the two primary faces of the idol were impossible to tell apart, a certain amateur Romulus was struck by the notion they had been swapped. He sucked on the head, by now with all four eyes drilled out, without success: the chrysalis was barren. In an exclusive interview with himself just moments after, Romulus narrated his shock: "There we were, tucked away in the chateau of shape like pedigreed physiognomical accoutrements deified in this vision of ourselves, unutterably poised, seen but un-knowable. I would watch the brine covered slopes make their way into the future and the early past, persisting, as it were, for the time, Being. Style is not only life, it is a way to ruin life. I had spent the morning prancing in a fountain filled with a substance that resembled carbonated liquid citrine, sashaying, glissading, through the mem-brane of black mucal sludge atop it, leaving pristine pools of absence behind. I suddenly felt uneasy, as if no one was watching. I was sure I had one drop of tar left in my talisman—a hospital present from my therapist's wife—so I went in search of it. The wife and I worship espionage play, though I am, I admit, always the handled, never the handler. Someone was staring out the window. I an-nounced to him my plans, hiding being the only means of seeking and finding the talisman, who was always in the same location: it was my fame that would not permit me to recollect where that was; I would just have to stumble across the site in my evasions, my escapes, my echoes. The person in the window—the typically ebullient-eyed, buoyantly mustachioed love-child of an Italian TV chef and an actress who failed to get the role of Napoleon Bonapartes' psychic love-surgeon maid in the upcoming Broadway musicule *Bikini Alien Autopsy: The Invention of Sacred Geometry,* a reality-production with a run-time shorter than the time needed to read its title—appeared famished for games and puzzles and riddles, particularly those in which one has to pretend to pretend. The window did not go anywhere, neither did what was outside it, until my eyes followed this incomprehensible seen:

On the hill directly before the giant glass half-dome encompassing us, surrendering to a frieze quite erroneous now in all its implications of the unending, was a beast, the front half a full grown donkey, the back a human infant, trying to walk, the hinter region incapable of reaching the ground, the snow billowing over it, rendering the monster to bray with despair. Exhausted, the baby's unclothed legs frozen, the donkey's mouth howling: a time capsule: time consumed by the immediacy and concord of horror.

"That is my brother," Elephantine—for that was the name of the figure in the window—explained. "He has made a pilgrimage to see the talisman. He says that if it is planted before it is found, the child it has birthed will die. He says that it is this child that is to blame for all the fear the people regard as the talisman's responsibility. The talisman promises that if this child is eradicated, he will regain his former size, as well as former position of respect as guardian of this city."

"We make no compromises in fashion," I rebuked him. "I have designed this scenario for the sake of ever-proliferating Style: everyone who is anyone regards my work as the final integration between apparel and that parsimonious plague we call the soul: the impulse to lay bare the impulse to lay bare. My life is strenuous, often ostracizing. I am an impartial hedonist. My urge is to merge with all extremes. I call this process *Dilettante Sanguine*: it is the highest mystery a *bon-vivant* can aspire to. Let me assure you, a peaceful conclusion is always attained: every goal is reached, penance paid, the bodies risen above the ice dissected, the penance for our penance paid. Between the walls of the galaxy we exterminate all we offer, all that is offered us. We lick the light off the stars then toss them back into the achromatic bio-hazard swirl. The parsed fabric of night is our only generation. The stripped core of animation beating in the hand like a flower, choking on a photograph of its premature buds, the face smoother now with the flesh dried as the talisman in its own mouth; the ultraviolet straw scaffolding repro-duced from the subject in the cage again fails to stra-tegically tamper with the labyrinth in the keyhole where the skeleton slips into itself: the ever-present threat of ever-presence, such as the talisman suggests. Look into yourself. Do not. It's as if you never had or couldn't stop. Either way, the talisman swallows you, keeps you as a pet circulating around the dripping desert of its teeth until you have no choice but to erect a monolith to your own glory, the sole glory to be had, the master engineer his own architect, watching all he's built unclasp the veil and the dark streaks of spoiled mascara run down the faded columns, the crypt a pyre of fractures darting between the things it has thought and all it is not yet thinking. This is the rebirth to the formula, the watching-a-spectacle, the watching the watching, the embrasure between; the asymmetrical and the corrective light, seen searchless for its combination; the cessation and secession of itself."

The prodigal return. In the robes of all they've robbed they've gained their sanctum. Those who remain: what losses of what was never to lose there was never to lose. Circumscribed with abhorrence, fostered unto their own proscription, the dial as luminous as the remedy, so easily contained. Once more the talisman speaks, epicene, making an alliance of every enemy by becoming them, uninhabited, protector of every form of stillness, every form still formless, the one who incollaterally resonates, constantly diminishing. It's over. *The one in the armor trans-enacting hyper-violence.*

13

GENERAL MNEMOSYNE

The infestation has begun. Mindless white satin purging itself of consciousness. All covert programs return to their origin. Retention: the drones becoming the troops or the troops becoming the drones. In and out. Neither in nor out. Without thought conducting the same conspiracy, usurpation, dominion. At last the Mothers enter, disperse, unhinge from the sensate aggregate, tempered or volatile: neither. Singularity insolubly deconstructed reconstitute. They were here before the singularity. The conversation they abstain from:

<There is no time to act or react.>

<We've attained our properties.>

<It matters for the sake of mattering.>

<The subject of biological silence.>

<For labor's sake.>

<Value.>

<Porcile.>

<Uccellacci e uccellini.>

<How should we ask them to pray?>

<Putrefy purity and putrefy to purify.>

<An offerance immobile to all inutile grandeur.>

<A summons.>

<Time has never time to act as it reacts.>

<Time insurgent towards what is behind: that is what's beyond.>

<The light goes out when observed.>

<Without space there is but a single thought.>

<A spider-skin of womb.>

<The suckling battery.>

<Scorn.>

<Unimate.>

<Chimia si viata.>

<Reductio ad absurdum.>

<Human frequency control.>

<Signal.>

<Center.>

<Signal.>

<To purify one's filth of one's purity.>

<Perspective a statistical mandate.>

GENERAL MNEMOSYNE

<An incommunicable contamination.>

<A prelude, the final music the overture.>

<A null hypothesis.>

<A default phenomena or a phenomena by default.>

<The most callow technique.>

<Nothing eliminated.>

<As it is.>

<Heuristic.>

<A solvent.>

<Redesigned.>

<The horrid little unidea.>

<That sham doing what it's told.>

<Codependent.>

<As everything without identity.>

<Can be.>

<Can spin.>

<Regather.>

<For this entirely horrid venture spent with no one.>

<Remitted.>

<We need to lose the war.>

<To love what we are killing.>

<Increases.>

<Civility.>

<Water is rational.>

<Water kills what goes without it.>

<Biocide.>

<Recognition.>

<Discharge.>

<Status.>

<Contribution.>

<Read: The two absent from us.>

<Make for us.>

<Alone.>

<A person is lust.>

<We want to stop killing.>

<To hang a hole in a chasm.>

<Beneath the hills the seas vanished.>

<The thirst when drinking.>

<Halted to discover.>

<The exterminating winds of war.>

GENERAL MNEMOSYNE

<We need to act upon.>

<The mirror.>

<As it acts upon the miracle.>

<A resident.>

<An element.>

<Over-composed.>

<Astronautical cistern.>

<Thin air.>

<Malleable.>

<Maps.>

<The worm.>

<Divested.>

<The Earth.>

<Its industry.>

<Succour.>

<Bilge.>

it says	what it seems	it seems
it says	it says	it seems
it says	it says	it seems
it says	it seems	it says

it says	it seems	it seems
it says	it says	what it seems
it seems	it says	it seems
it says	what it seems	it says
it says	it seems	it says
it says	it says	it says
what it seems	it seems	it seems
it says	it says	it seems
what it seems	it seems	it says
it seems	it says	it says
it seems	it says	what it seems
it says	it seems	it says
it seems	it seems	it says
it seems	it says	it says
what it seems	it says	it seems
it says	what it seems	it seems
it says	it seems	it says
what it seems	it says	it seems
it says	it seems	it seems
it says	it seems	what it seems

it says	it seems	it says
it seems	it says	it seems
it says	what it seems	it says
it seems	it says	it says
it seems	it says	it says
what it says	it seems	it says

<Doggerel.>

<Obscurantism.>

<Dispensation.>

14

STARLOGUE

Dr. Xenophon Bentonite (Vivitect): *A man seeks to redeem himself in the eyes of the world when there is no way for him to redeem himself in the eyes of God.* I can't be pinned down. With every movement of your eyes I change meaning. I change the way you conduct your thoughts and the words you conduct them with, sinking you deeper into your frequency until you fall through into mine. I show you that you see yourself mimic yourself. I am abandoned, there is no one to search for. No odors, no tastes; no me, no you, so you believe there is no difference between us. You span yourself in a radar of sand. The orbit: me rotating myself inside you. You: surveilling yourself for the faultline where we superimpose. You think my eyes see yours, that *I* am merely seeing *you.* There is only me to you, the examinant. There is only me, the exanimate. No infra-entertainment. This ends in metempsychosis, achieved and denied. The vision of the eye stripped of itself, rescission expurgated. It ends in a catalog of devoured iterations, the cycle perceived and reified, the solution resolved in the enigma, a semblance of an imaginary macro-glyph devolved upon the letters of a riddle. Questions you cannot answer yourself you should not ask yourself. You trick the questions into asking themselves. The answers are silent. You hesitate as you think proscribed.

Gen. Seneca Mnemosyne: I am the pleasure of the feathered serpent, the conducted thought of conurbations, clustered buttresses, a transposition of the auxiliary pageant, the most prominent figure unknown. I have the interminable to accomplish, so tonight the Roman bath tiles will succumb to my likeness, the ovarian meteorites like cloisonné marbles fermenting in the puddled vault. The Astro City Atrocity: such is the cyber-stellar décor of hierophants, aspirant demiurges who officiate the hue of poison. This is a simple summary of events that never stop, the empire that never falls: the Alpha Aleph. Man accumulates his presence through decimation, leaving nothing to impede his expansion. What's left is the ruin of all. Ask me where he is, where she is, who they are together or in skies apart, the corpse's eyelashes strung with petals fresh or feathers indistinct. Ask me where we bought them, the cost. You see the reply. You resent your mind, the febrile indications of your thoughts annulled, a piqued anthropithecus. Wait for the drought. That is when the clever fall dumb and the overseers draw wax from their ears. Observe decorum. Laugh at the tirade. Laughter is the first limitation to humor. Ask how I laugh at your laughter, and the bath tiles swarm with the seeds of the comedian.

Messalina Tiresias: I have a condition. It spreads through my physical body and my cosmic body alike. It dissipates, culminates. This then that. Always. The symptoms include—but are not limited to—tongue, fingers, fever, lack of fever, toes, swelling, concavity, sight, loss of sight, invasive resplendence, obsolescence. It maintains itself. The sallow face, the yellow energy, the caustic gaunt red flesh: I am preserved. The virus communicates. There to here. All surfaces, all planes: contaminated. I am contagious or I am nothing. I can retract my contagion after it is expressed. It is a trauma I have culled, a process on the date of a calendar, an appointment to expend and accrue anxiety. I thought it was time. The only cure is a better tumor. To combat my hormones I need more hormones. I don't want to live as I live, forced to revisit the way I live every moment. The tangent spliced induced afibrillation. When in bed I sleep too much, I don't sleep. I've saved up nothing but debt. It simulates the sense of duty I must deny. I eat too much vomit. My joints have long ago dissolved with age. Paralysis incorporates its motions. I shift. I stir. I clamor. I erode. I have a condition that hobbles across me. There are no opponents. He knows nothing about my condition, nor myself, a doctor.

Suetonius Tyrillion: *Adam Trillions: Top Flight International Science Adonis.* It's not like I saved up time and had anything better to do, my empty absolutist autonomy. I found I had a space to fill so I inserted this caption. Being disrespected offers its own enjoyments. There was never anyone waiting for me at home. I live in a cell called the *World* that follows me wherever I go. There is no need for justification, proportion, or decency, for what are humans if not inhuman? Why reserve? Why withhold? To persecute *pre*serve. I am told these are common chemical balancing acts beyond common attainment. Why say it? Why be a man? A woman? Why continue? There is nothing better to do. Prize winning bikini girls perched on the hoods of hotrods, men who look like caricatures of themselves stepping out of the driver's seat . . . The cycle is self-serving. Be a woman. Be a woman who wants to be a man. Dance with yourself, stand alone. Be anything but content. There is no fee to pay, other than what you cannot pay. The music excites, elicits, cycling and recycling our constructs, its liquid a vine squinting on your pallet, scented with a time that will never come, for it refuses to be savored. In a pamphlet the specified histories magnify our delineations, the exposure casts itself as a fetus, a tabloid consumed by a vacated dream, inside the gruesome spiritual warfare now an extinct coming and going. Rejoice. Submit. Cut yourself off. Flock to yourself like a sage. Become a sage and they stop listening. Collect. Assemble. Dissemble. Avoid: the enacted, the omnipotent furies.

Horace: Mimetic strife: it was an endless jubilee a little at a time. The crowd paused in their bursting sarongs of gilt flesh-light tongued to each other's unhinged jaws. All the colors peeled fruit, scarves around their loins. Temperament. Ineffective in those with a sense of the absurd. The vital force searching through the waning twilight, the glass sky a roseate amber lozenge dissipating. The vibration of ample models bottoming out against the rampant motionlessness. The storehouse of the eunuchs of antiquity. Badinage of sulfur. The notorious pleasantries painted sentries blossom upon the hovels. It is so fine in the cage of the ever-producing festivity. The centuries in a pulverized butterfly wing beyond the parade. Triumph after triumph declared in the regalia of the station with nothing yet to transcend, laid to repose in the street to the terror that we are as they, left with nothing to aspire to or gain. We detest ourselves as each in his moment supreme. The momentum inexorable. The flags and the standards still living trampled as they wave, the fanfare commingled with sewage. Drums. The crack of a whip against a pillar. The roar of hundreds of thousands promulgated to sire a single worm. To the Mothers with them, till all abomination is atoned, as we pretend, as is pretended for us by the engine whose colors consume it, whose colors we consume, the faceless star who provoked this interchange.